COUNTENANCE
OF TRUTH

ALSO BY SHIRLEY HAZZARD

FICTION

Cliffs of Fall
The Evening of the Holiday
People in Glass Houses
The Bay of Noon
The Transit of Venus

NONFICTION

Defeat of an Ideal

VIKING
Published by the Penguin Group
Viking Penguin, a division of Penguin Books USA Inc.,
40 West 23rd Street, New York, New York 10010, U.S.A.
Penguin Books Ltd, 27 Wrights Lane, London W8 5TZ, England
Penguin Books Australia Ltd, Ringwood, Victoria, Australia
Penguin Books Canada Ltd, 2801 John Street,
Markham, Ontario, Canada L3R 1B4
Penguin Books (N.Z.) Ltd, 182–190 Wairau Road
Auckland 10, New Zealand

Penguin Books Ltd, Registered Offices:
Harmondsworth, Middlesex, England

First published in 1990 by Viking Penguin,
a division of Penguin Books USA Inc.

1 3 5 7 9 10 8 6 4 2

Portions of this book originally appeared in *The New Yorker* as
"Reflections: Breaking Faith."

Grateful acknowledgment is made for permission to reprint an excerpt
from "The Quest" from *Collected Poems* by W. H. Auden, edited by
Edward Mendelson. Copyright 1941 and 1969 by W. H. Auden. Re-
printed by permission of Random House, Inc., and Faber and Faber Ltd.

LIBRARY OF CONGRESS CATALOGING IN PUBLICATION DATA
Hazzard, Shirley.
Countenance of truth: the United Nations and the Waldheim case /
by Shirley Hazzard.
p.   cm.
ISBN 0-670-83230-8
1. Waldheim, Kurt.   2. United Nations.   3. Austria—Presidents—
Biography.   I. Title.
DB98.W28H39   1990
341.23′24—dc20   89-40422

Printed in the United States of America
Set in Bodoni Book

SHIRLEY HAZZARD

COUNTENANCE
OF TRUTH

The United Nations and
the Waldheim Case

VIKING

In memory of Ivan Morris

And when Truth met him and put out her hand,
He clung in panic to his tall belief
And shrank away like an ill-treated child.

—W. H. Auden

ACKNOWLEDGMENTS

I should like to thank those former or present members of the United Nations staff who have helped me in this work. I also wish to express my gratitude to the late Leonard B. Boudin, and to Jack Sargent Harris and Theodore W. Kheel, whose statements appear in the text; and to the late Norbert Guterman, with whom I first discussed certain themes of the book. My thanks go to Amanda Vaill, Scott Edward Anderson, Theodora Rosenbaum, and their colleagues at Viking Penguin Inc., and to my literary agent, Julie Fallowfield of McIntosh and Otis Inc., for friendship as well as for exemplary professional care.

In thanking Robert Gottlieb and the staff at *The New Yorker*, it gives me pleasure to record my particular debt to John Bennet for his support, advice, and kindness; and to Martin Baron, who, with his colleagues of the Checking Department, gave untiring and inspired attention to an exigent task. These persons, together with Elizabeth Pearson-Griffiths, provided inestimable assistance and solidarity.

As always, my thanks go to Francis Steegmuller, who once again shared the experience of the work.

ACKNOWLEDGMENTS

I should also like to express, in connection with this book, my appreciation of the services of the New York Public Library, the Libraries of Columbia University, the New York Society Library, and the Zionist Archives and Library of New York City.

S.H.

COUNTENANCE
OF TRUTH

1

"NATIONS FROM TIME TO TIME assume that it is allowable and inevitable for them to fall upon each other on some pretext or other." So the historian Jakob Burckhardt wrote, more than a century ago, at the onset of the Franco-Prussian War—warning that "the most ominous thing is not the present war, but the era of wars upon which we have entered." In the same fateful year of 1870, Gustave Flaubert wrote to George Sand: "Within a century, shall we see millions of men kill each other at one go?" The acceleration and incoherence of social and economic change, the transformations wrought by scientific discovery, the growth of populations, and of their enfranchised discontent—all these raised, in the minds of reflective men and women, a sense of moving toward some dread culmination, propelled by factors never before present in human experience. Over these apprehensions, the discrepancy between the narrow thinking of statesmen and the huge scale of the mounting crisis cast—as it does today—the shadow of a prodigious incongruity.

The two conflicts that, within the first half of the twentieth century, brought unprecedented slaughter, destruction, and grief to some of the most enlightened and loveliest lands on earth caused a large segment of articulate humanity to question whether the phenomenon of war was indeed warranted and inevitable. This doubt—which had, we may suppose, seized the obscure survivors of countless immemorial conflicts—was voiced, after the great war of 1914–18, in societies drawn closer by rapid communications, by a large measure of literacy, by diffusion of democratic precepts, by international commerce and enhanced material aspirations; and by a wave of common fear and shared suffering. For the first time, apprehensions were expressed by large populations whose "universal" suffrage would soon be extended to tens of millions of the "opposite sex"—of women, traditionally removed from the instigation and prosecution of wars, yet in the forefront of war's victims. The creation of the League of Nations, in 1919, as the first modern instrument for global mediation, could not have occurred without that aroused popular instinct for self-preservation.

That this new challenge to governmental concepts of national power was not sufficiently resilient or sustained to achieve any proper realization of its hopes does not alter its significance. A rational collective impulse is not, in the human story, so commonplace that it can be dismissed as incidental. Much sincerity was expended in the inauguration of the League; but that sincerity did not, among the League's supporters, take dynamic or durable form; while, on the part of governments, it was never conspicuous, and soon gave way to bad faith. More fundamentally, the creation of a large organization, in seeming emulation of a parliament, was never deeply questioned as a response to the world's need. It is the impulse of our century, with its nearly religious belief in magnitude, to fling an institution into every void. But the vacuum in the management of modern nations derived, at the time of the League's founding, not from a lack of bureaucratic machinery, but from the absence of greatness, and even of judgment, in public men—whose folly had been evidenced in the relentless continuance of a calamitous and unnecessary war. Favorable change could have come about only through an infusion of intelligence, magnanimity, and active imagination into places of power, and by a demand for concentration rather than mere expansion. Instead of a vast enterprise installed in labyrinthine offices and grandiose council chambers, stifled by procedural entanglements and weighed down with numbers, there could have been proposed a smaller organism where ability, with its immeasurable powers, might be directed toward the alleviation of humanity's distress. The ponderous unwieldiness of the League contrasted tragically with the ruthless velocity of events between the wars, encouraging the moral dereliction of its member governments, the timidity of its leading officials, and the dispersal of its authority into bureaucratic gestures; and playing a capital part in the predetermined failure of this first venture into organized internationalism.

In 1945, public engagement with the revived idea of a "world organization" appeared at first less passive—intensified, as it was, by a cumulative revulsion from slaughter and destruction; by the shock of systematic atrocities; and by the invention of the atomic bomb and its use by the Allies as a decisive weapon of war. In Europe, too, there was wide realization that civilized life could not materially or spiritually survive another such onslaught of self-inflicted wounds. It was felt that the League of Nations had foundered not because the idea was intrinsically unworkable but because the League itself had been created by governments as a weak instrument, enervated by formalities and debilitated at its inception by a limited frame of reference and by the aloofness of the United States. Before the Second World War had come to an end, plans were yet again set forth by the victorious Allies for a new organization, which would now ideally include not only the United States and the Soviet Union but, ultimately, every established government on earth; and which would play a role in bringing new nations to birth and maturity. Such an institution would exist, above all, for the prevention of war, and for moderation of outdated and hostile manifestations of nationalism. Whereas, however, a large segment of humanity was stirred by a new, if unformulated, need to participate in this larger concept of statehood, the politicians were not ready. The United Nations organization was created in the League's image—still larger, wealthier, and more diffuse; its potential for political action so reduced as to be realized only by exceptional, and exceptionally determined, individuals. Thus the public impulse for self-preservation was for a second time acknowledged by the world's leaders, nominally appeased, and rendered all but innocuous to national objectives.

On each of these occasions in recent history, the immediate requirements of nationalism succeeded in diverting the energies of internationalists to the maintenance of institutions where nationalism would reign, virtually silencing an important expression of public opinion and expectation. The

United Nations emerged as a temple of official good intentions, a place where governments might—without abating their transgressions—go to church; a place made remote— by agreed untruth and procedural complexity, and by tedium itself—from the risk of intense public involvement. The United Nations enterprise was not made accountable, or even intelligible, to the peoples of the world; and has been interpreted to populations by their governments.

In 1945, therefore, the new organization's hope for achievement lay almost exclusively in the realm of personality. The possibility of defense of principle, on the public behalf, by leading officials of the organization itself had not been excluded from the United Nations' constitution. In the conception of the mightiest member states, that possibility appeared not as a hope to be defended but as a threat to the exercise of unbridled national power: in the light of events, it may truly be said that it inspired terror. Such a show of apprehension on the part of politicians might have been understood, and grasped, by the organization's leaders, as a tactical advantage and a source of strength. But this possibility, too, was circumvented by the unlawful selection, by governments themselves, of compliant men to lead the world's new venture. Since the moment of the United Nations' inception, untold energies have been expended by governments not only toward the exclusion of persons of principle and distinction from the organization's leading positions, but toward the installation of men whose character and affiliations would as far as possible preclude any serious challenge to governmental sovereignty, or dynamic intervention on behalf of the organization's stated aims—men who would agree to the institution's remoteness not only from public scrutiny but "from beholding the bright countenance of truth." The election of Kurt Waldheim as the fourth Secretary-General of the United Nations was both a symptom and an inevitable result of that process, whose reality has now been exposed to public view; and whose history is told in these pages.

In 1945, the Preparatory Commission of the United Nations urged that in directing the new organization "the Secretary-General should take the necessary steps to ensure that no persons who have discredited themselves by their activities or connections with Fascism or Nazism shall be appointed to the Secretariat." In 1948, this provision was included, as a General Assembly directive, in the comprehensive regulations for the new international civil service issued by the first Secretary-General, Trygve Lie; and survived four years. In December, 1952, the stipulation disappeared, apparently without opposition from member governments, U.N. leaders and supporters, or the press. The erasure was, however, noted at the time by lawyers representing a group of U.N. employees dismissed without cause by Lie. The circumstance and its context are recorded in the Brief on Behalf of Nineteen Applicants presented in the United Nations Administrative Tribunal in 1953. That brief is an essential document for any informed assessment of the history and present condition of the United Nations. The formative episode it recounts prepared the ground, more than any other single factor, for the later degradation of the office of United Nations Secretary-General.

In 1949, four years after the United Nations' founding, Trygve Lie contracted a written secret agreement with the United States Department of State whereby, in violation of basic liberties and of the United Nations Charter, applicants for and incumbents in U.N. Secretariat positions were "screened," without their knowledge, by United States agents. Although directed in the first instance against American citizens—who, numbering about two thousand, then constituted approximately half of the U.N. headquarters personnel—the influence of this clandestine agreement extended to U.N. employees of other nationalities, and permeated U.N. specialized agencies abroad, such as UNESCO and the Food and Agriculture Organization. The policy confirmed in the agreement—a policy aimed not only at excluding convinced internationalists from the international civil service but at aligning that service with current and parochial attitudes in the United States—had been established well before its written formalization, with effects apparent to the staff. On March 11, 1947, at Lake Success, where the infant organization was provisionally installed, a mass meeting of U.N. employees confronting Lie had informed him, through a young Frenchman who was their spokesman, "There is a total lack of confidence and understanding between you and the whole staff." The following day, in a front-page account of the event, a New York *Times* U.N. correspondent, A. M. Rosenthal, reported, "They asked for permanent contracts to give them security. They sought a clear-cut policy on dismissals. They demanded a definite end to appointments and promotions through outside contacts with delegations and ambassadors." These calls for adherence by U.N. leaders to the sworn principles of United Nations service would be fruitlessly reiterated by staff representatives and internal management studies for the next forty years.

In an angry and characteristically emotional response, Lie availed himself, in turn, of an argument that would thenceforth be used by U.N. senior officials to silence inquiry into malfunction and malpractice at the organization: "Everything you say will be used against this organization by the enemies of the United Nations." An insistence that the United Nations should be shielded from realistic appraisal and that its significant errors should be denied or dissembled even within the institution itself thus took hold in the U.N.'s earliest years, precluding any candid exchange with the public, and sparing the organization the need to demonstrate resolve and utility before the world. Support of the United Nations accordingly came to be understood as a sentimental acceptance and propagation of the organization's self-proclaimed image, without informed challenge to its deep realities; and the interest of inquiring minds was consequently withdrawn.

In 1949, the year of Lie's secret agreement with the State Department, an internal investigation was conducted into charges of anti-Semitism within the Secretariat administration. While establishing—as Lie reported in January, 1950—no evidence of "an overt act of anti-Semitism," the U.N. board of inquiry found that "there were, however, administrative actions of an irregular character which had the appearance of unfair discrimination against the complainants and certainly caused the complainants to suffer unjustly." Five dismissed employees were reinstated, and others were reassured of their positions. Shortly afterward, in

March, 1950, some of these persons were again dismissed, on the fictitious ground that their posts had been abolished. And, again, these actions arose from Lie's covert subservience to United States political pressures.

That the international civil service should be denied independence at the outset, and by the intervention of its most powerful democratic member state, was a conclusive defeat for any practical realization of the United Nations concept. The fateful experience of the League of Nations had demonstrated that the enduring worth of an instrument for, in the words of the U.N. Charter, "the prevention and removal of threats to the peace" would require an objective and highly professional civil service, defended by a vigorous Secretary-General whose own initiatives were constitutionally authorized—a service nurturing, as its main support, the wide public attention and good will extended to the United Nations in its earliest years. An entitlement to public trust, through demonstrated and sustained moral authority, would, in turn, provide such a Secretariat with the stature and cumulative power to resist governmental pressures and to exert a favorable and intelligent influence in world affairs. As Evan Luard, a historian of the United Nations, has written, the new organization "would clearly be able to secure law and order only by maximizing intangible influence of this kind."

In 1919, at the inception of the League of Nations, John Maynard Keynes had acknowledged the validity of this same belief: "The League will operate, say its supporters, by its influence on the public opinion of the world. . . . Let us pray that this be so." Keynes went on, however, to warn against a merely sentimental application of this hope, advising that strict and energetic vigilance would be needed to activate the beneficent provisions of the League's constitution, lest the League "become an unequalled instrument for obstruction and delay . . . an unwieldy polyglot debating society in which the greatest resolution and the best management may fail altogether to bring issues to a head against an opposition in favour of the *status quo*."

The positive view of the Secretariat's potential, framed in the aftermath of the League's failure and incorporated into the U.N. Charter, was briefly borne out during the years of Dag Hammarskjöld's best diplomatic initiatives, when the public interest aroused around the world by his active endeavors immeasurably strengthened the Secretary-General's hand in his dealings with governments and played its part in his unanimous reëlection to a second term. Hammarskjöld's political interventions were, however, individual in conception, and ceased with his death—as did the popular attention they had engendered. Without a resourceful leader, and without the complementary support of a skilled and disinterested civil service, the United Nations could only, as its founders foresaw, become a hugely magnified forum for governmental tactics and transformations, and for national propaganda, before which the world's public would remain unrepresented and largely helpless. The Secretariat and its chief officer were charged with representing, through the defense of principle, the public interest.

In seeking to guarantee "the highest standards of efficiency, competence, and integrity" in the new international staff—with only a subsidiary provision for "due regard" to its geographical composition—and in prohibiting improper dealings between governments and the Secretariat which might modify or thwart that objective, the drafters of Articles 100 and 101 of the Charter were doubtless aware that the Soviet bloc in particular among the organization's members would, while reluctantly, and only nominally, subscribing to such principles, place its chosen and supervised candidates throughout the Secretariat. At the outset, however, Soviet employees were few. And it was reasonable to suppose that adherence to the relevant Charter undertakings, by "Western bloc" governments which constituted the overwhelming majority of the fifty-one original member nations, would outweigh and eventually isolate violations. As Joseph P. Lash would observe, writing in the—then liberal—New York *Post* on December 12, 1952:

> While it is conceded the Soviet bloc maintains an ironclad control over their nationals on the UN staff, no one believes Soviet practices should necessarily become the models of international conduct.

At the U.N.'s founding, good faith with the Charter on the part of most members was assumed in respect to this fundamental issue of staff independence. And when the question was raised of an employee's possible conflict with the special interests of his government, it was asserted that the experience of the League of Nations demonstrated that there was no practical difficulty in this matter except in the case of Fascist states.

That presumed good faith was promptly breached with the installation, by the great powers, of chosen national candidates as immediate deputies to the Secretary-General—a violation committed with the ill-omened acquiescence of Trygve Lie. The establishment of an independent international civil service was still, however, envisaged and indeed taken for granted by the organization's supporters. What was not foreseen was that the United States—then and long thereafter dominant in all United Nations affairs, and custodian not only of the organization's purse but of its best hopes—would at once conspire to abrogate this fundamental undertaking of the United Nations Charter. Still less, that the first Secretary-General would make himself a main party to that conspiracy.

2

THE SECRET AGREEMENT OF 1949—the text of which is appended to the verbatim record of the Internal Security Subcommittee hearings of the United States Senate in the autumn of 1952—was implemented at the United Nations by Lie himself, a Norwegian, together with a group of his senior officers, most (but not all) of them Americans. It was the particular concern of Lie's Assistant Secretary-General for Administrative and Financial Services, Byron Price, who had been a wartime director of the United States Office of Censorship and a postwar executive in the American film industry. As the secret agent of the United States government within the United Nations leadership, Price devised and controlled the U.N.'s administrative policies throughout the organization's formative years. Although his name scarcely appears in U.N. studies and memoirs of the period, the significant power over the Secretariat was in his hands.

Trygve Lie, who had served as Foreign Minister with the Norwegian government-in-exile in London during the Second World War, had been elected Secretary-General after other candidates foundered on disagreements between the Western and Eastern blocs—which is to say, between the governments of the United States and the Soviet Union. In his later memoirs, Lie would describe his consternation at being selected for such an office:

> I had been nothing less than catapulted into the Secretary-Generalship of this new international organization. . . . It was a challenge beyond my wildest dreams; but it was a nightmare as well. I hardly dared to think of the days ahead. Instead, I asked myself again and again, Why had this awesome task fallen to a labor lawyer from Norway?

Crude without forthrightness, devious without astuteness, Lie was above all deficient in ethical perception. The choice of such a figure to inaugurate the office of United Nations Secretary-General in itself expressed the shallow intentions of the great powers in regard to the new organization.

Under a "cover plan"—so characterized by State Department witnesses, in the autumn of 1952, before the Internal Security Subcommittee chaired by Senator Pat McCarran—a show of propriety was maintained in official correspondence between the United States mission and the United Nations administration, while American directives for dismissals of U.N. personnel were presented through "informal, confidential, word-of-mouth channels." The name of the designated victim, according to Byron Price's account, was accompanied only by "oral evaluation, which consisted many times of a single word, such as 'reject,' 'questionable,' or 'incomplete.' " In a memorandum of December 23, 1952, to the State Department, arising from the McCarran Subcommittee hearings, Price stated that "adverse evaluations, when received, have been wholly unaccompanied by security evidence or information on which the evaluations were based." In the same vein, John D. Hickerson, Assistant Secretary of State for United Nations Affairs at the State Department, and negotiator and supervisor of the secret agreement, informed the McCarran Subcommittee:

> It is true that United Nations officials expressed the wish from time to time that they could have detailed information or evidence. However, to my knowledge, there was never at any time a statement from the Secretary-General that the secret procedure was unsatisfactory in the sense that he would not act on the basis of the comments being supplied and that these comments were useful only as a basis for further investigation. If there had been, we would have taken steps to try to work out a new procedure.

Hickerson had been a United States adviser at the Dumbarton Oaks preliminary conference on the United Nations, in 1944; and, in 1945, at the organizing conference in San Francisco, where the Charter principles were framed and confirmed.

It was the apparent hope of State Department officers, in recounting their illicit dealings with the United Nations administration, to demonstrate to the McCarthyist faction the Department's determination to frustrate the internationalist undertakings of the Charter. The desire of the inquisitors, in turn, was to show that the clandestine arrangements between the United States authorities and the U.N. Secretary-General did not go far enough.

Under the secret agreement, at least forty United Nations

15

employees of United States nationality were dismissed, with damaging publicity, from 1951 to 1953, all of them having, as far as I can determine, superior efficiency ratings at the U.N. and none of them being charged with an offense. Colleagues and staff representatives who came to their defense found their own United Nations employment terminated or conclusively blighted in consequence. Prolonged suspension of contractual security by Lie and Price left many of the dismissed without possibility of redress. Those whose contracts had been confirmed before that hiatus, however, eventually received substantial compensation from the Administrative Tribunal, the appellate instrument of the United Nations system itself, meeting abroad and internationally composed of distinguished independent jurists. The organs of the United Nations thus showed themselves in open conflict on this basic issue.

In 1953, American anger over the compensation awarded by the Administrative Tribunal to eleven former U.N. employees precipitated referral of the matter, by the U.N. General Assembly, to the International Court of Justice, at The Hague, for an "advisory opinion" as to the necessity of making the designated payments. Recipients of the awards were meanwhile vindictively recalled before the United States Internal Security Subcommittee, the record of their interrogation being made public at length in *U.S. News & World Report* of October 16, 1953. The World Court, in an opinion delivered in 1954, upheld the ruling of the Administrative Tribunal. The payments were made only in the following year.

Briefs attempting to justify these and similar dismissals before the Tribunal had been drawn up at the Secretariat under the direction of the United Nations chief legal officer, Abraham Feller, an American. Hampered by the absence of reason and due process in his own and the Secretary-General's actions, Feller had also labored under the necessity of concealing the real motives for the terminations and their instigation by the government of the United States. The case presented on the Secretary-General's behalf—which seeks to justify arbitrary actions by the Secretary-General against his staff—is often grotesquely inappropriate to a declared center of legal standards (as exemplified in the administration's stated claim that "the question of the motive for a failure to give a new contract is legally immaterial, even if there were in fact an improper motive"). The appellants themselves were represented by a succession of distinguished jurists, who included Telford Taylor, Frank Donner, and the young Leonard Boudin.

Looking back at these events, Boudin said in 1989:

> The U.N. aspect of the McCarthy era was as irrational as, for example, the denial of passports for political reasons. Neither had even the surface justification of the irrational and unconstitutional security clearance system for U.S. government employment. It was both ludicrous and immoral for an international organization to enter into a secret agreement with a national government to deny international employment to United States citizens because of their constitutionally protected right of association.
>
> The lengths to which the U.S. government went regarding the staff members were illustrated by its resistance to paying the damage awards and by the fruitless referral to the International Court of Justice; and by similar U.S. actions in F.A.O. and UNESCO.

17

The staff officials involved, from all these agencies, were the best international civil servants, and their removal represented a permanent loss to the public—just as the purge of distinguished teachers [in the early nineteen-fifties] from the New York City schools constituted a lasting deprivation for our children. The dismissed U.N. officials, after suffering obloquy and economic loss, eventually advanced in other fields. One had to meet and know them to be moved by their nobility of character and their courage under the extraordinary attack by their United Nations employer and by a series of U.S. government institutions operating in tandem or unison. In many ways, they found their equal only in the tribunal of international jurists—the U.N.'s Administrative Tribunal, then headed by Mme Suzanne Bastid.

Studies and memoirs of the United Nations that allude at all to this fundamental matter omit, almost without exception, the experience of those who suffered under it or contested it on principle. The personal accounts and documentary evidence of these men and women at the center of the drama, and of the jurists who supported or vindicated them, the essential summary contained in the Brief on Behalf of Nineteen Applicants, the moral significance of the findings of the Administrative Tribunal, and the revelatory archive of the staff's resistance, all these have been persistently excluded from U.N. histories. Yet those abundant records shed, on every aspect of the events and on the personalities involved in them, a strong light quite at variance with the shaded official illumination.

3

THE NUMBER OF international employees who, in a steady draining, left the United Nations system during its first decade because of intimidation, indignation, or disillusion may be estimated at several hundred. Some were encouraged to resign with special payments; sixty others were removed as part of an "efficiency survey," carried out in 1952, the records of which were immediately destroyed. Also in 1952, a panel of three jurists appointed by Trygve Lie to advise him on the "loyalty" question pleaded, as justification for the Secretary-General's departures from his Charter obligations, the special requirements of "the host country." The composition and findings of this panel did little to restore the confidence of the Secretariat.

In the autumn of that year, the presidential campaign between Dwight D. Eisenhower and Adlai Stevenson stimulated the excesses of the McCarthy movement. In the days preceding the presidential election, diverse elements of the investigating committees, meeting in New York, interrogated a number of United Nations employees. At the Secretariat, it was first rumored that Lie's—by then manifest—secret agreement with the United States government would soon be revealed by State Department officials before the McCarran Subcommittee, a disclosure that Lie's tenure could not long survive. Although Lie had, on occasion, made emotional reference, behind closed doors, to a claimed readiness to resign his office, that recurrent offer had been considered rhetorical. Now, however, large events carried the day.

Unnerved by the public illumination of his covert policies, yet ever more acquiescent to McCarthyist demands, Lie was in fact obliged, on November 10, 1952, to tender his resignation to the General Assembly, in an atmosphere charged with tension. Three days later, Abraham Feller, Lie's chief legal officer and close associate, committed suicide at the age of forty-seven, driven—as both his widow and Trygve Lie publicly stated at the time—by the same events. Speaking to the American Philosophical Society on the evening of Feller's death, Ralph Bunche, then principal director for trusteeship at the U.N. Secretariat, made what appears to have been his only public criticism of "American pressures on the United Nations." (In later years, Bunche stated privately that pressure on his own position from the investigators had deterred him from taking a stand against the McCarthyist persecutions.) Shaken by Feller's death, Trygve Lie himself briefly spoke out in the same vein—an extravagance for which he soon apologized. Less than a month earlier, however, the Secretary-General's legal representative at the McCarran hearings, Oscar Schachter—a senior legal officer of the Secretariat—had fervently thanked the subcommittee for its "spirit of complete fairness," adding, "I should like the record to show that in no case did the Secretary-General interpose any objection to a question presented . . . to any witness in the United Nations."

In 1987, in his book *The Eighth Case: Troubled Times at the United Nations,* describing the experience of McCarthyism at UNESCO, Julian Behrstock, a former official there, recounted a discussion with Oscar Schachter more than thirty years after these events: "In our interview he characterized Lie as 'craven'—but he apparently shared the Secretary-General's position as to the need to propitiate the American investigators."

In a letter regarding Feller's death published in the *Times* on November 16, 1952, Telford Taylor went to the heart of the matter, asking, "What voice has been raised . . . to point out that the notion of political conformity within this staff can, and surely will, be applied to the grave disadvantage of the democratic cause? . . . There has been, so far as I know, no official comment to help set the matter straight."

Those of Lie's senior colleagues who were not his accomplices in the secret agreement maintained public silence throughout those crucial years. Among the heads of department, Hugh Keenleyside, a Canadian in charge of the Technical Assistance Administration, came forward within the Secretariat to defend his staff. Many criticized Lie's actions behind their hands, aware that audibility had its price. So far as I can discover, no one who openly condemned the conduct of the administration in this episode subsequently prospered in the organization. Others, who would, like Lie himself, later speak and write of "the witch-hunt," deplored, during the events themselves, the staff opposition to Lie's illegalities.

21

In the prevailing political climate of the country, the inevitable exposure, in the McCarran Subcommittee meetings of early December, 1952, of Lie's clandestine arrangement with the State Department aroused only brief press attention and little public indignation. A handful of embattled civil libertarians and journalists took note, however, of the fatal significance of the events—among them, Leon Edel, then writing regularly in the *Daily Compass*. Otherwise, outrage was scarce in the American press, and citizens were not encouraged to understand what they had lost. In Europe, however, prominent newspapers called on Western leaders to defend the Charter principles—an official intervention made drastically unlikely by postwar conditions of European economic and strategic dependence on the United States. (In November, 1952, certain British and Canadian officials of the United Nations Secretariat called privately on Anthony Eden—then, as Britain's Foreign Secretary, attending the U.N. General Assembly—to urge his defense of the international civil service. Eden told them he was unaware of any violation. Since, in 1945, Eden himself had briefly hoped for the Secretary-Generalship, this incident may possibly indicate the course he would have followed in office. Discussing, in his memoirs, those November days at the U.N., Eden makes no mention of those events, traumatic for the United Nations, that took place immediately after his arrival.) Writing in *Le Monde* on November 22, 1952, Maurice Duverger proposed the removal of the United Nations from the United States, pointing out that, had an analogous collaboration been revealed between the Secretary-General and the Soviet Union, it would have generated an outcry across America.

22

The Soviet bloc, which, for its part, had adopted a boycott of Lie over United Nations involvement in the Korean War—and which had no stake whatever in the independence of the U.N. Secretariat—watched this episode of Western folly with every appearance of sardonic unsurprise.

It is difficult, if not impossible, to find, in the published literature concerning the United Nations, any discussion of the secret agreement of 1949. The tendency seems, rather, to invert Lie's actual role in the McCarthy era—a distortion first presented by Lie himself, in his memoirs published in 1954. Writers who exclude all reference to the secret agreement have suggested that Lie's resignation arose from Soviet displeasure over his role in the Korean conflict—even though the Korean events dated from June, 1950, while Lie's withdrawal occurred at the height of the McCarthy attack on the United Nations, in the autumn of 1952.

In his autobiography, *A Life in Peace and War*, Brian Urquhart—for many years a leading spokesman for the Secretariat—touches briefly on the era of McCarthyism at the United Nations without mention of the secret agreement. Urquhart gives his view that "Lie tried to defend his American staff by cooperating with the American authorities in investigations to clear those who were under suspicion. In normal times this might have been the best course to follow, but times were not normal. Lie was caught in an impossible situation, for in cooperating with the procedures designed to clear the accused members of the Secretariat he whetted the appetite of the witch hunters, gave credence to their charges, and lost the confidence of his staff." No such picture emerges from the massive documentation of this issue, which overwhelmingly confirms that—as stated in the Brief on Behalf of Nineteen Applicants—"the Secretary-General of the United Nations not only has been subjected to these effective [American] pressures, but indeed has initiated, cultivated, and sought them out." The records of the McCarran Subcommittee hearings for 1952 and 1953 make equally clear that those investigations, like other inquisitions of the period, were aimed not at clearance but at victimization. Concealing its collusion with the United States authorities and heedless of the moral and statutory rebuke of the U.N.'s own tribunal, the United Nations administration conducted and expressed itself throughout those years as the implacable adversary of its own staff—initiating a schism that would be destructively perpetuated throughout the organization's subsequent story. For a young person such as myself, arriving in America at this time and eagerly enlisting in the United Nations' service—where I would remain, in a junior position, until 1961—these events marked an epoch. The mood of grim occasion in which they occurred was unforgettable; and Trygve Lie himself spoke of it as "the atmosphere of Greek tragedy."

In 1953, a prominent American appellant to the Administrative Tribunal, Jack Sargent Harris, was awarded compensation of forty thousand dollars with respect to his dismissal by Trygve Lie—in view, as the Tribunal stated, of his "outstanding professional competence" and "the very limited and specialized nature of his profession as anthropologist and African specialist whereby the opportunities of further employment are rare" and "the fact that he joined the United Nations at the special request of Mr. Ralph Bunche, Director of the Trusteeship Division, thereby terminating his previous career." (Seven years later, as the United Nations embarked on its mission in the Congo virtually without specialized personnel, Dag Hammarskjöld would concede that "the Secretariat . . . does not dispose of a sufficient number of highly qualified senior officials.") Harris's career as an anthropologist was completely destroyed by this episode, which—in the frenzy of the times—left him no possibility of governmental or academic employment. Rebuilding his life, he eventually prospered as an industrialist. In 1989, he related, for this account, his experience in those years at the United Nations:

In 1946, I was invited by Dr. Ralph Bunche to join him at the Department of Trusteeship at the United Nations. At the time I was an anthropologist on the faculty of the University of Chicago. Bunche said that he wanted me because of my work in Africa, and especially in West Africa; and, in February, 1947, I was appointed to the U.N.'s Division of Trusteeship, of which Bunche was Director. I was subsequently awarded tenure there as a Senior Officer. My work at the U.N. was concerned with the improvement of social and economic conditions of peoples in the African Trust Territories, and with the attempt to establish viable bases for their political development toward independence. It was an exciting period at the United Nations. In the Secretariat we felt that we constituted a truly international civil service. The work was challenging, demanding, stimulating, and we believed that we were contributing to the noble principles of the U.N. Charter.

That period ended abruptly. Many of the American citizens employed by the U.N. were called to testify before Grand Juries and Congressional subcommittees on the broad question of loyalty to the United States government—in other words, we fell victim to the witch-hunt during what is now known as "the McCarthy era." In December, 1952, I myself was dismissed from my United Nations post as a result of my appearances before the Senate subcommittee appointed to investigate the administration of the Internal Security Act. We were stunned to find that Trygve Lie not only refused to protect our status as international civil servants but actually pandered to the F.B.I., bowed to the hysteria of the times in the United States, and participated in inflicting the indignities that we suffered. And what was our crime? We had invoked the protection of our Constitution against unlawful harassment. The Senate subcommittee attempted to assume powers that rightly belonged to the courts, but we were denied the safeguards inherent in normal court procedure.

Clearly, by his conduct in this affair, Trygve Lie compromised the integrity and independence of the international civil service.

The consequences of our departure from the United Nations, I am told by former colleagues, were insidious and far-reaching. Motivation and spirit were gravely affected. Pressures of various countries on their nationals in the Secretariat became more insistent. A number of Secretariat staff withdrew or took early retirement rather than continue to work in a cynical and restrictive situation lacking much of its former meaning.

Lie remained in his post for more than four months after tendering his resignation. (His effort to continue there indefinitely has been recounted by James Barros in his study *Trygve Lie and the Cold War*.) In the new year of 1953, he "welcomed" the executive order of the departing President

Truman by which, in complete violation of the U.N. Charter, an exhaustive official screening of all Americans in United Nations positions was instituted.

The uncontested establishment of this national clearance nullified the Charter concept of an independent and effective civil service and inflicted untold damage on the potential of the United Nations. Other member governments would thenceforth—at first by degrees, and subsequently in a flood—also install their nominees in virtually all significant, and in many insignificant, U.N. posts. Hundreds of meaningless and costly positions would be created throughout the leadership of the U.N. system for the sole purpose of accommodating national candidates—some of whom, devoid of qualifications, were unwanted in their homelands for political motives, while still others arrived trailing rumors of incompetence or scandal. The work of field missions would, on occasion, be similarly encumbered by such superfluous emissaries, dispatched to lucrative senior field assignments from a headquarters that had found their presence burdensome. In 1978, the fourth Secretary-General, Kurt Waldheim, would inform his unhappy staff that "the General Assembly has made it clear that the composition of the Secretariat with respect to the geographical distribution of the staff is the over-riding factor"—without reference to the contrary mandate of the Charter. By the nineteen-eighties, the New York *Times* would report the view of "one Western Ambassador" that "You try to get as many posts as possible for your own nationals. This is wrong, but everybody does it." And the salaries of senior members of the U.N. service would in a number of cases be supplemented, in another reversal of the

Charter articles, by large subsidies from their respective governments (one official receiving, for instance, a U.N. salary of a hundred and twenty thousand dollars a year while accepting from her government an additional annual payment of eighty thousand dollars). Each ensuing violation has been condoned by successive Secretaries-General, whose sworn obligation and public claim it is to defend the Secretariat from just such interventions. ("This book is my religion," the fifth Secretary-General, Javier Pérez de Cuéllar, told the *Times* in 1982, pointing to the Charter.)

The provision, inaugurated by Trygve Lie, for "full field clearance" by United States agents of all American candidates for U.N. appointments was confirmed, with superficial adjustments, by Dag Hammarskjöld in the first year of his incumbency. With some procedural modification, it was to remain in force for over thirty years. In September, 1983, as the result of a sustained challenge to its legality by Dr. David Ozonoff, a candidate for employment at the United Nations World Health Organization, the clearance was ruled unconstitutional by a United States District Court judge. Dr. Ozonoff had been represented by Leonard Boudin. An appeal of the court's ruling by the United States government was disallowed in 1984. And in 1986, following the upholding of a subsequent legal challenge to the procedure, the national security clearance requirement for American applicants to United Nations positions was at last withdrawn. This victory was, significantly, the result of persistent defense of right by private citizens and their counsel, unassisted by the extensive legal apparatus incorporated in the United Nations. While the confirmation of fundamental principle was historic, and indispensable to the design of any future body that may replace the present United Nations, its benefits could scarcely be felt in an institution now heavily staffed by the chosen candidates of one hundred and fifty-nine member governments.

Early in 1953, however—in the inaugural year of the new clearance procedure—a branch office of the United States Federal Bureau of Investigation was installed, with Lie's approval and with the blessing of the new United States representative at the U.N., Henry Cabot Lodge, Jr., in the United Nations headquarters building, for purposes of surveillance, interrogation, and fingerprinting of all Americans on the international staff. The F.B.I. agents remained in the Secretariat, on international territory, throughout the first year of Dag Hammarskjöld's incumbency, departing—as Hammarskjöld confirmed in 1954, in response to a reiterated staff inquiry—only on completion of their task. Again, no United Nations leader or supporter publicly contested the F.B.I. presence, or rose to the defense of a junior employee, of United States nationality, who, having challenged the propriety of these investigations on U.N. premises, was dismissed from her post by Hammarskjöld. As Conor Cruise O'Brien observed, in 1964, "On what might be called the McCarthy issue, Hammarskjöld bowed, more gracefully and inconspicuously than Trygve Lie, but bowed none the less, to prevailing American opinion."

The abhorrence felt by Secretariat employees for this new invasion of their rights was evidently incomprehensible to the United Nations administration and its legal officers. "What I could not get across to them," Oscar Schachter told Julian

Behrstock in the nineteen-eighties, "is that the investigation was concerned only with loyalty and that they had nothing to fear in replying to these personal questions."

The United States, satisfied with its ascendancy, neither then nor later acknowledged its leading role in the destruction of the quality and impartiality of the United Nations Secretariat. Although the adverse consequences, as they began to appear throughout the entire framework of the United Nations, were bitterly deplored by American critics, no effort was made to trace their origins. As the chairman of the Foreign Relations Committee of the United States Senate, J. William Fulbright, would point out in *The New Yorker* in 1972, "Having controlled the United Nations for many years as tightly and as easily as a big-city boss controls his party machine, we had got used to the idea that the United Nations was a place where we could work our will."

Senator Fulbright's candor was exceptional, and unfamiliar to the public. In a contrasting, and prevalent, vein, in 1985, Senator Daniel Patrick Moynihan, denouncing Soviet abuses of the international civil service as "forbidden by the United Nations Charter," could declare with little fear of knowledgeable contradiction, "We keep to the rules. They do not. And they despise us because we do."

Accountability, that source of institutional health, had been excluded from United Nations experience; and, along with it, indivisibly, the stimulus of direct public engagement and response. "It is not a United Nations Organization," Aleksandr Solzhenitsyn was to say, in his Nobel address in 1970, "but a United Governments Organization." In offering itself

as the mere creature of its member governments, the United
Nations system entered a state of arrested moral development, marked by the habitual emblems of immaturity:
demands for approval, hostility to truth, and an incapacity for
individual or collective self-questioning. The organization
emerged from its definitive trauma of the McCarthy years—
which had encompassed the forced resignation of its principal officer, the exposure of his chief deputy as a national
agent, and the suicide of his legal adviser, together with a
host of less conspicuous tragedies—with no admission of
error, no gesture of atonement, no effort at self-recognition.
No official inquiry into the motives and actions of Lie, Price,
and their leading collaborators was even proposed; or into the
exact circumstances leading to Feller's suicide, which remain obscure today. The attitudes and policies reflected in
Lie's revealed collusion with the United States authorities
were never examined for their wider implications and possible influence on world affairs. An official proclamation of
standards of conduct for the international staff, drawn up in
1954 under Dag Hammarskjöld, compounded the schism
between a mistrustful personnel and an autocratic administration; and, since it did not address the misconduct of the
Secretariat's leading officials, or the institutionalized consequences of their violations, was irrelevant to the story of the
organization's first nine years.

No just venture could prosper in such conditions. But the
United Nations was particularly unsuited to a reversal of
founding principles which made a paradox—or mockery—of
the organization's insistent claim to moral standing. The
United Nations had been established as a center of stan-

31

dards, charged with maintaining and extending the benefits of liberty and order around the world. Integrity as well as practical service was explicit in the terms of Secretariat employment, necessitating individual moral courage as well as organizational distinction. By its very anxiety to annihilate the Secretariat's independence at the outset, the U.N.'s most powerful member state had shown keen awareness of the potential that organized internationalism might develop, in a convulsed, contracting, and nuclear world, should its valid endeavors progressively capture the public interest.

Speaking, in 1936, of "the spacious conception" of the League of Nations, Winston Churchill had stressed the imponderable public power touching such an enterprise: "You must not underrate the force which these ideals exert. . . . One does not know how these seeds are planted by the winds of centuries in the hearts of the working people." Despite the constitutional authority—embodied in the opening words of the Charter—of world citizenry over the United Nations, intelligent public engagement has been the least nurtured element of all the organization's latent potential. The public has been regarded as a passive and uniformly unenlightened audience for U.N. proclamations, and as a sounding board for the vanity of U.N. officials. The possibility of progress toward peace rests, nevertheless, with active enlistment of what Dag Hammarskjöld called "the final, least tangible, but perhaps most important new factor in diplomacy: mass public opinion as a living force in international affairs . . . the expression of a democratic mass civilization that is still in its infancy, giving to the man in the street and to group reactions a new significance in foreign policy." A momentous demonstration of this public power took place in Eastern Europe in the autumn of 1989.

When the United Nations was inaugurated, it was not imagined as an entity with concerns other than the public good. In 1952, however, to facilitate the arbitrary dismissals required by his secret pact with United States authorities, Trygve Lie sought and received from the U.N. General Assembly the revised staff regulations that, together with other portentous changes, omitted the former prohibition against recruits having discreditable "connections with Fascism or Nazism." These revised rules also stated, in respect to employment in the international civil service, that "the Secretary-General may at any time terminate the appointment if, in his opinion, such action would be in the interest of the United Nations." Patently a formula for cloaking improprieties, the allusion to unspecified "interest" initiated, also, a new stage of United Nations history. In its years under Lie and Price, the Secretariat had acquired concerns and purposes at variance with ethical and legal standards prevailing in what would thenceforth be persistently referred to at the United Nations as "the outside world" and "the real world"— expressions employed not in regretful consciousness of the organization's detachment but in a spirit of exclusivity, and of condescension to the uninitiated remainder of humanity. The denial, at the bidding of member states, of due process within the institution itself would be reflected in a pitiless forfeiture of U.N. obligations to defend the human rights of oppressed individuals and unsupported minorities around the globe.

In 1952, "the interest of the United Nations" encompassed

in the new official phrase was supremely related to the power—political, psychological, and financial—of the United States over the organization. By 1975, however, the sources of pressure, and of the urge to appeasement, had diversified. In refusing to appeal to the North Vietnamese authorities on behalf of millions of refugees trapped in the terminal chaos of the Vietnam War, Secretary-General Kurt Waldheim declared, "It is not in the interest of the United Nations to get involved in this political aspect." Featuring those words in its Quotation of the Day, the New York *Times* reported, on April 3, 1975, that Waldheim "made it clear that he believed a public appeal by him to the Communists in Vietnam to allow refugees to leave would be 'counterproductive.' " The *Times* went on to say, "Mr. Waldheim, in a rare show of emotion, expressed bitterness over accusations published in the United States that he was biased and was sensitive to Communist pressures. 'This is unfair,' Mr. Waldheim said, his face reddening. 'I have to weigh very carefully the interests of all the 138 member states.' " On the same theme, according to the *International Herald Tribune* of April 8, 1975: "Mr. Waldheim said he had no intention of resigning because of criticism directed against him. 'The criticism comes from the West exclusively,' he said. 'From no other part of the world. On the contrary, the rest of the world seems satisfied.' "

We must wonder to what specific "interest of the United Nations" Waldheim was alluding in this matter, and which particular governments among "all the 138 member states" preferred to suppress an appeal for mercy on behalf of these refugees. (In ensuing days, Waldheim claimed he had been misquoted by the *Times*; but the newspaper's reporter had preserved the record of discussion.) While presenting his action in a context of governmental requirements, Waldheim ignored the audience best qualified to assess such a decision—the suffering populations themselves.

In a previous episode regarding large numbers of helpless fugitives, the League of Nations and its officials had refused to involve themselves in Hitler's persecution of German Jews, choosing to regard the matter, after 1933, as an internal question not touching the jurisdiction of the League. In 1935, the League of Nations High Commissioner for German Refugees, James McDonald, resigned over that issue, pointing out in a public statement that the Covenant of the League of Nations—an instrument analogous to the subsequent Charter of the United Nations—specifically empowered the League to intercede in such calamities, and adding, "I cannot remain silent. . . . When domestic policies threaten the demoralization and exile of hundreds of thousands of human beings, considerations of diplomatic correctness must yield to those of common humanity." It is probable—although, in those early years of Nazism, not assured—that intercession by the League would have proved ineffectual. Events might well have moved inexorably to their same conclusions—but not, for the League, with the same moral disgrace. The League's refusal at that time to deplore the inhumanities of Nazism sealed its dishonor as well as its enfeeblement, leaving it unable to cite in afteryears even an inspired gesture during the crucial event of Europe's modern story; and provided precedent for similar dereliction at the United Nations.

In April, 1975, no Secretariat leader felt obliged to dissociate himself from Waldheim's statement on the "counter-productivity" of an immediate appeal on behalf of refugees. "The best the United Nations can do," an unidentified U.N. official told the *Times*, "is preserve its impartiality and usefulness for the future." The United Nations, which had been virtually silent on the Vietnam conflict throughout the preceding decade, thus forfeited, in the crucial hour of change, an opportunity to influence the fortunes of a displaced people, whose tragedies would thenceforth multiply.

4

"LOYALTY," which—as the slogan, cynical or hysterical, of the McCarthyist movement—had dominated the national experience of the United States during the United Nations' formative years, was an early preoccupation of the Secretariat leadership. The undefined "interest" of the United Nations formally promulgated in 1952 had already demanded attestations of an allegiance distinct from those loyalties to principle and public service required by the organization's constitution. And, as is usual in such abuses of a call for "loyalty," those who steadfastly adhered to the declared standards of the institution were stigmatized and expelled. Lie and Price had repeatedly insisted on an automatic fidelity on the part of the staff to the person of the Secretary-General, rather than to the provisions of the Charter, or to the truth. On October 2, 1950, in response to a staff attempt to bring administrative violations to the attention of the General Assembly, Byron Price stated, in a menacing circular distributed throughout the Secretariat, "If any specific cases of disloyalty to the Secretary-General appear, there will be no choice but to call them to his attention." In 1951, as Trygve Lie prepared to dismiss a

37

young staff representative who had protested Lie's violations, he declared, "If the staff in New York want to make trouble, the issue will be a simple one; it will be a question of either loyalty to Mr. Robinson"—the Vice-Chairman of the Staff Committee—"or loyalty to me."

The "termination"—in the fateful U.N. idiom—of this employee, a Canadian, was the fourth dismissal by Lie and Price from the staff leadership of seven elected members, of whom, by 1953, only one would remain. The action conclusively intimidated organized staff resistance, which was now to stay subdued for a generation. Awarding damages in this case, the Administrative Tribunal commended "the high qualities possessed by the Applicant" and "the shortage of persons of his knowledge and experience," which guaranteed his prompt reëmployment in his own country.

In March, 1953, a debate was held in the U.N. General Assembly arising out of a report on personnel policies presented by the departing Trygve Lie. (Of this mendacious document, a Soviet representative stated, with undeniable accuracy, "There is no truth whatsoever in the assertion in Mr. Trygve Lie's report . . . that 'it has always been [his] policy . . . to uphold the international character of the Secretariat, and to resist all pressures from whatever source which could have the effect of undermining its independence as defined in the Charter.' The procedures followed in the Secretariat indicate the exact opposite.") In an intervention historic in the context of the Secretariat's later fortunes, the chief French delegate, Henri Hoppenot, who had been Lie's most eloquent critic among governmental representatives, called for immediate reversal of abuses that, with their "menacing consequences," precluded the creation of a valid international civil service. Proposing, on a note of urgency, specific remedies—all of which would be ignored—Hoppenot proceeded to address the ominous development, within the United Nations leadership, of the call for an unreasoning "loyalty" that would override propriety and justice:

> An end must be put to everything that seems to make the Secretary-General's post an autocratic one, to everything that tends to make the staff subject to the whims and caprices of their superiors and makes careers—and even employment—dependent upon blind obedience to such absolute power.

Critics of the French government's subsequent indifference to the United Nations—to, in de Gaulle's phrase, *"ce machin"*—take no reckoning of early French efforts to save the organization from its formative wounds.

Originating with Lie and Price, the call for unquestioning subservience to an office and a personality gained decided authority during the tenure of Dag Hammarskjöld, to whose temperament the concept was congenial. Hammarskjöld was forty-seven when, in April, 1953, he came to the United Nations from a ministerial post in the Swedish Foreign Office. He was fifty-six when he died, on United Nations service, in a plane crash near Ndola, in Northern Rhodesia, on the evening of September 17, 1961—the anniversary of the day on which, in 1948, Count Folke Bernadotte, Hammarskjöld's fellow-Swede and U.N. mediator, was assassinated in Jerusalem. The only Secretary-General to stimulate, by personal and attestable effort, universal interest in the organization's potential, he is also the sole United Nations leader whose personality sets him apart as a figure of wide interest and arouses a wish—as yet unsatisfied by biographers and commentators—to learn its sources and deeper manifestations. He is, too, the single notable instance of a man whose powers were extended and fulfilled in the United Nations ambience, which more commonly acts as a swift reductive.

Born into a prominent Swedish family, Hammarskjöld received the liberal education of his class, whose manners and northern outlook he reflected. He had, like Goethe, a stern, cold father and a tender, spirited mother, to both of whose memories he was faithful. In him, these parental elements did not coalesce into creative genius but evidently remained disparate and conflicting. His own best writings—in particular, the brief, late memoir, *Castle Hill*, that recalls the fortress setting of his early years at Uppsala—testify to a fastidious sensibility. There is also much testimony to the moodiness that showed itself in frigidity, in offensiveness, and in a habit of condescension that swelled, in the closing phase of his life, toward imbalance. Beyond the culture of his upbringing, Hammarskjöld had a love of poetry and an affinity for all the arts, together with maturity of intellectual thought and expression—attributes that astonished in the United Nations circle, where they had by then become extremely rare. His natural reserve was tinged in his last years with an apparent wish to propose the clues to his own enigma; and his journal, *Markings*, posthumously published, is less an account of the moral progress of an intensely private soul than a self-conscious and at times histrionic rendering of such a journey. Its illumination is therefore limited and often inadvertent. The entries show not only awareness of a hypothetical reader but an underassessment of that reader's powers of penetration.

Biographers of Dag Hammarskjöld writing in the two decades following his death apparently did not seek out with diligence the mentors or companions of his youth; or test Hammarskjöld's own recalled experience and self-assessment against the records and recollections of others. More recently, so far as I am aware, no fresh or surprising evidence has been brought forward. Time, and much testimony, has thus been lost, and a merely general impression of Hammarskjöld remains, without color or dimension. The largest work on Hammarskjöld, published by Brian Urquhart in 1972, is almost exclusively—although not exhaustively—devoted to his official performance as Secretary-General. Urquhart himself explaining, in his Foreword to that volume, that "I have in fact, written the book throughout from the point of view of an international civil servant," and going on to say that the book, "written mainly from Hammarskjold's point of view as Secretary-General . . . is intended mainly to give an account of Hammarskjold's Secretary-Generalship and of his own concept of his role."

Hammarskjöld's private life has therefore remained obscure—the more curiously since, in leaving us a journal that reports his innermost thoughts and feelings, and in envisioning that journal's publication, Hammarskjöld himself invited consideration of his personality. The question of his sexuality, in particular, has either been treated as sacrosanct or left to idle speculation. Briefly commenting on this matter in his study of Hammarskjöld, Urquhart gives his view that "stupid

41

or malicious people sometimes made the vulgar assumption that, being unmarried, he must be homosexual, although no one who knew him well or worked closely with him thought so." In his later memoirs, Urquhart states, on the same theme,

> I worked closely with Hammarskjold for eight years, as did many others. None of us ever saw the smallest evidence or justification for this story, which was assiduously peddled by people who did *not* know Hammarskjold and who, for one reason or another, resented him. . . . There is nothing particularly novel or unusual about homosexuality, but the rumors about Hammarskjold always struck me as vulgar, and sometimes self-serving, attempts to demean an exceptional and unusual person.

We need not agree that interest in this human aspect of a public man is necessarily stupid, malicious, or vulgar; nor that discovery of a homosexual tendency—which has been characteristic of many talented and productive lives—would demean or diminish Hammarskjöld's stature. It might rather seem—since sexual nature is a central influence in any life—that such an interest is among the duties of a serious biographer, whose principal motive is a quest for truth. To a detached observer, there do appear to be suggestions of possible inversion in Hammarskjöld's temperament.

Brian Urquhart had not perhaps reflected that, in the case of a later Secretary-General, he himself, together with the United Nations senior circle, angrily repudiated, for many years, reports of Kurt Waldheim's concealed life, only to find themselves mistaken. Of this later, and truly distasteful, episode concerning Waldheim, Urquhart himself has said:

I was one of his under-secretaries and one of those who dealt with him most. I had always taken completely, as everyone else did, at face value what he said about his war record. I was shocked to discover that it wasn't the truth.

The coincidence of Hammarskjöld's own need for arduous dedication and his abrupt selection for a position of assigned but disregarded moral leadership was greeted by him as a virtually religious responsibility. Chosen for the post, by United Nations member governments, as an obsessive bureaucrat whose self-effacing officialism appeared to guarantee obedience, he brought instead to his U.N. task the fervor of vocation, the vigor of released energies, and an exaltation both productive and problematical. What made this possible is—like almost everything of deep meaning in his experience and nature—yet to be discovered. Much is undoubtedly still to be learned, too, of his official actions and of the influences, interior and external, that bore on them.

Hammarskjöld's contribution to history derived from his ingenious development, as he gained confidence in his U.N. role, of a basis for independent political intervention by the United Nations Secretary-General. Demonstrated most effectively in regard to the Suez crisis of 1956, the concept was also expressed in a continuity of prognosis and initiative which created an intelligent presence in world affairs; and this longer perspective may be observed in Hammarskjöld's intercessions in Asia, where he foresaw the makings of catastrophe. The possibility of such a role, placed by the U.N. Charter at the disposal of the Secretariat leadership and laid waste by Trygve Lie, required for its affirmative use exceptional human qualities of a kind that Hammarskjöld at his best possessed.

The formidable aspect of Hammarskjöld's character, with its conscious superiority, did not markedly favor his work at the United Nations; and his distinction was to some measure achieved in the face of it. Hammarskjöld displayed an autocrat's imperviousness to defects of his own policies; an autocrat's incapacity for delegating authority; and an autocrat's indifference, also, to conditions of individual or collective injustice that did not directly touch his imagination. The United Nations, which might—and, in pursuance of its own proclamations, ought to—have led the postwar world in the defense of human rights, made no advance in that field during his tenure, when countless thousands of unavailing appeals gathered dust in U.N. archives. United Nations responsibilities toward the status of women—the organization being, nominally, the global custodian of women's rights—were similarly allowed to stagnate, while the U.N. administration's attitude was expressed, then as now, in obdurate discrimination against female employees. There was no woman among Hammarskjöld's senior deputies; and, during his term of office, only isolated instances existed of women in notably responsible positions at the Secretariat. (According to personnel statistics issued by the United Nations in July, 1989, two women are now employed in the Secretariat's most senior category, as contrasted with fifty-one males. In the immediately subordinate category, the figures are, respectively, six and ninety-four. The imbalance is "corrected" only in the most junior and clerical grades.) Throughout his life, Hammarskjöld's chosen associates, in his work as in his private life, appear to have been—like his correspondents and memorialists—almost exclusively male.

During his first year in office, Hammarskjöld sought and largely obtained from the General Assembly administrative powers, that, invested in the Secretary-General, were at variance with the intentions of the Charter toward the international civil service. (His attempt to modify the authority of the Administrative Tribunal was acceded to only in part; but the standing and importance of that body declined.) Hammarskjöld's actions in this respect were condemned in a searching study, by Claude Julien, of erosion of rights at the United Nations, published in *Le Monde* on November 19th and 20th of 1953—a study that may be read with much interest today, when history has exposed the inadequacies of successive Secretaries-General. In this course the new Secretary-General was supported by his deputies, although with isolated expressions of dissent. Guillaume Georges-Picot, the respected senior French member of the Secretariat, strongly protested such a concentration of administrative power in the Secretary-General. An imperious communication of March, 1954, from Hammarskjöld to his senior officers, quoted by Brian Urquhart in his study, *Hammarskjold,* makes clear that Hammarskjöld's demand for "a spirit of true teamwork, with the loyalty that such work requires" was to be interpreted as a call not simply for a proper measure of coöperation and order, but for obedience to a leader who regarded disagreement with his views on significant questions as "symptoms of a tendency to put other interests before those of the United Nations and—in some cases—of what I must call personal

45

disloyalty." Georges-Picot resigned from the Secretariat at the end of 1954.

The renewed insistence on unconditional loyalty to a personality, whose requirements are equated with those of the United Nations, again illustrates the removal of the U.N. service from democratic systems. Such a demand might have raised questions in an advanced national civil service, where it could have been appealed. In this central matter, as in others, Hammarskjöld's inaccessibility to rational opinion is disquieting. Byron Price had departed—leaving his administrative precepts entrenched, as it seems, forever. Hammarskjöld's retention of the remaining senior officials, predominantly of American nationality, who had either supported or declined to oppose Lie's abrogations, and his failure to recruit or retain persons of talent, or to expel sycophants, were part of a striking remoteness from realities by then besetting the U.N. service. They may presumably be understood, also, as indications of intolerance for any strength of character that his temperament rejected as competitive.

Like most of his deputies, Hammarskjöld had no sustained contact with the staff body, and his pronouncements concerning the organization's condition and morale were misconceived. The abstractions set forth on paper as administrative policy during his U.N. years did nothing to mitigate the alienation of a body of persons deprived of a merit system, uncertain of their rights, intimidated by procedures of surveillance and by the network of secret files maintained on each employee by the organization itself; and conscious, above all, that adherence to the explicit principles of their appointment would result in their victimization or dismissal. The separation of United Nations affairs from normal legal and ethical accountability had left the international staff quite without the "effective protection from external pressure and internal domineering" called for as a matter of urgency by Henri Hoppenot of France in March, 1953. Many of those fifty-one original member states against whose interference the U.N. Charter had provided were bound, by watchful populations in their own lands, to an observance of basic rights under laws and regulations far more exigent than the policies applied within the United Nations.

Some realization of basic disorder was forced on Hammarskjöld near the end of his life, by the scope and complexity of his expanding political initiatives, which exposed the deficiencies of the Secretariat: "There is," he acknowledged, in his eighth year of office, "not enough of a diplomatic tradition or staff with training in political and diplomatic field activities to meet the needs which have developed over the years." That late awareness was subsumed, with his death, into the tenebrae of Secretariat affairs.

Conor Cruise O'Brien, writing shortly after Hammarskjöld's death, likened the meetings between Hammarskjöld and his senior officers to those "between a youngish headmaster and a bright sixth form." Within the staff, the attitudes of Hammarskjöld's colleagues toward their Secretary-General were, at the time, characterized even more astringently. Yet the analogy of a school—still ingenuously invoked on occasion by the organization's spokesmen—remains pertinent to the pervasive immaturity, the petty ascendancies and tyrannies of Secretariat life.

In a bizarre episode, which was to culminate in the appar-

ent suicide of a senior official who had opposed his orders on
a claim of principle, Hammarskjöld set forth his views within
a long personal letter of dismissal, of July 3, 1958, published
almost immediately as a United Nations press release:

> It is further my view that any moral reservations which
> might have prevented you from obeying my instructions do
> not ameliorate the impropriety of your conduct as a member
> of the Secretariat in refusing an order by the Secretary-
> General relative to official papers. It is my view that if you
> considered your clear official duty to acknowledge my
> authority in Secretariat matters to be in conflict with your
> private moral convictions arising from an unauthorized
> assumption of authority, it was your duty to resign from the
> service.

This official, a Dane named Povl Bang-Jensen, had, following an assignment concerned with Hungarian refugees,
refused to relinquish papers identifying activists in the Hungarian uprising of 1956, for fear—as he contended—that
the confidentiality of such documents could not be protected
at the international Secretariat. His position was repudiated
by Secretariat leaders, who later asserted—possibly with
foundation—that the man was unbalanced (leaving, in turn,
the question as to why he had then been entrusted with a
vital humanitarian mission). Aside from its particular mer-
its, the case served as a forum for Hammarskjöld's views,
expressed with despotic ferocity, with regard to the unre-
flecting submission he required from his staff.

A disciplinary body composed of senior members of the
United Nations circle reproduced Hammarskjöld's attitude in
their censure of this "defendant," declaring that "the staff

member must accept the findings of the higher authority or leave the service." This psychology of subordination, in which "moral reservations" were unlikely to be raised and all too likely to be punished, had its origins in the Secretariat's traumatic early years, whose lessons it ignored. Undiscriminating allegiance to a series of fallible personalities was ever more aggressively proposed, and meekly accepted, as a virtue. That such "loyalty" could become, in the upper ranks, a cloak for pusillanimous cronyism and that it might involve betrayal of the public trust were dangers ostensible but unexamined. In 1982, an admiring article in the New York *Times Magazine* concerning Brian Urquhart, then the Secretariat's senior Under-Secretary-General, reported that "though impatient with protocol and strong on improvisation, he is an organization man, intensely loyal to the institution and to its current chief, whatever his private reservations may be." With only the rarest exceptions, this definition of loyalty was applied unreservedly by the United Nations senior circle until the exposure, in March, 1986, of Kurt Waldheim's deceptions.

When a concept of institutional allegiance entails a forsaking of the righteous who, like James McDonald at the League of Nations, speak out from a larger responsibility to humanity and history, and to themselves, it will—whatever its immediate shrouding in contemporary excuse—be challenged at last by the independent destiny of events; and adversely judged by posterity.

5

AMONG THE NEW INTERESTS of the United Nations, material rewards assumed greatly increased importance for the senior staff—becoming from the time of Hammarskjöld's death, and with the growing affluence of the Western world, an always prominent and often paramount consideration. This was a result of diminished satisfaction and stimulus in the work itself, which now seemed to require some more tangible form of compensation. The early idealists who in applying to the United Nations had, in their eagerness to serve, scarcely inquired about their salaries had long since been eliminated. The exhortation of the architect Le Corbusier to the U.N. Headquarters Commission in 1946 that the United Nations should "not become 'great' like Babylon" was unremembered. From the onset of the nineteen-sixties, the habits and thousand annual entertainments of the United Nations General Assembly increasingly recalled a picture by Courbet, *The Return from the Conference*, in which a procession of carousing priests, dispersing from a church assembly, scandalizes a local populace. (Of this painting, later cut to pieces by a religious zealot, some photographs survived a police seizure of negatives in 1867.)

The extravagance of governmental representation at the United Nations set the tone of Secretariat expectations. In 1945, the Preparatory Commission of the United Nations had linked material benefits to the hypothetical qualities of the organization's future leaders, recommending that "the salary and allowances of the Secretary-General should be such as to enable a man of eminence and high attainment to accept and fulfil with dignity the high responsibility of the post. Similar considerations apply to the other principal higher officers." Although large payments were consequently declared necessary in order to attract recruits of exceptional ability, such persons were in practice seldom sought or valued by the organization; and might not, in any case, have made wealth a first consideration. An eagerness not only for high salaries and allowances but for individual ex-gratia payments, amounting on occasion to several hundred thousand dollars, stimulated, during the second Waldheim administration, the corrupt sale of certain profitable posts within the Secretariat, and the apparently uncatalogued arrangement of national subsidies to numerous employees, many of whom are, in a further violation of the U.N. Charter, seconded from national administrations to which they will return. The incompatibility of the organization's material practices with its stated aims intensified the alienation of the U.N. system from "the outside world," both at administrative centers and in the field. Although it contributed heavily to public skepticism toward the United Nations, immoderation was defiantly magnified with the passage of years.

Press reports concerning the United Nations' "regular budget" refer mainly to funds committed for administrative needs, and exclude the far greater operational costs of the U.N. system. The annual overall budget of the U.N. has, of recent years, been informally estimated at six billion dollars. However, I find it impossible to establish a reliable yearly total for the U.N.'s attestable overall expenditures, which appear to be vastly in excess of that sum. The organization informs me that no comprehensive figure can be provided. And piecemeal calculation cannot hope to include with accuracy the costs of every affiliate, subsidiary, and ad-hoc undertaking of the U.N. system; or to encompass the complex expenses of the U.N.'s financial institutions, the World Bank and the International Monetary Fund. So far as I am aware, no attempt has ever been made to assess the further extended financial commitment of member governments in maintaining within their foreign ministries bureaus of United Nations affairs and in participating, with a large diversity of offices, personnel, and counterpart expenditures, in United Nations projects and meetings around the globe. It is my impression that no one knows even the approximate cost, to world citizenry, of the United Nations enterprise. (An analogy—frequently drawn in public statements by U.N. officials—between the cost of the United Nations and that of the New York City Fire Department is at best fanciful: the budget of New York City's Fire Department for the fiscal year of 1990 was $662.8 million, a small fraction of acknowledged U.N. expenses.)

In June of 1979, an exposition by Ronald Kessler, in the Washington *Post*, dealing with the U.N.'s finances brought denunciation from both the United Nations and the U.S. State Department. Charles W. Maynes, then Assistant Secretary of State for International Organization Affairs, conceded that the *Post*'s figures were accurate but claimed, according to the *Post*, that the intricate nature of the United Nations system—by which a cumbersome administrative structure is reproduced, and jealously guarded, in each of a dozen specialized agencies, and in adjuncts such as the U.N. Development Programme—precluded assessment by outsiders.

Following the *Post*'s study, *U.S. News & World Report* published, in September, 1979, an article dealing with the allocation of expenditures within the U.N. system. With reference to material conditions for the senior categories of "the 44,000 persons" then permanently employed by the United Nations, the article stated, "President Carter is the only official in the U.S. government who is higher paid than dozens of U.N. officials." This appears to be a correct summation of the financial status of Secretariat leaders in the latter phase of the Waldheim administration. The official total of United Nations staff was given, in July, 1989, as 51,130, exclusive of many thousands of employees holding short-term contracts or serving as local recruits with U.N. field offices.

The siting of the United Nations headquarters in a city that sometimes perceives luxury and prominence as an index of achievement had encouraged the organization's excesses. The cloud of commentators and social aspirants who hovered about the embassies and principal officers of the organization would hardly have clung to them in more modest, if more exemplary, conditions—in which, indeed, few U.N. officials would have continued to serve. With the advent of Kurt Waldheim, emphatic importance was attached by the Secretary-General himself to the visible rewards and precedence of office—ostentation playing its part in the uncritical approval extended by the U.N.'s organized adherents to both the man and the institution. The transfer to United Nations custody of a town house at No. 3 Sutton Place, donated by Arthur A. Houghton, Jr., as a permanent official New York residence for the U.N.'s chief officer and his family, was completed in July, 1972; and Waldheim was the first occupant. This well-intended gift conclusively defined the Secretary-General's position as one of wealth and social prominence. Waldheim's three predecessors had lived at private addresses of their own choosing that provided some association with normal life. Shortly after his election, Hammarskjöld had expressed, at a press conference, his hope to strike "a proper balance between my wish to help the press and serve the public, on one side, and, on the other side, a strong personal desire to be able to work—and live—as much in quiet as possible." The Burmese schoolmaster and diplomat U Thant, who succeeded Hammarskjöld, had largely avoided U.N. festivities, preferring his domestic privacy on the city's outskirts. By contrast, in the Waldheim era, the Secretary-General's house became the culminating point of the social and material aspirations now associated with the United Nations. For their part, the organization's senior officials evidently chose to assume that a show of wealth supported by public funds in no way impaired their claim to speak for the destitute and suffering throughout the world—a situation recalling the comment of Cato the Censor on the supposed holy powers of the ancient soothsayers known as haruspices: that he wondered how one haruspex could look another in the eye without laughing.

The waste of public funds by the United Nations has been an expression, merely, of a far greater waste of the organization's opportunities and human resources. The latent power of the U.N. concept has always resided in the public confidence it might generate by high performance and demonstrated integrity. To that unrealized possibility, financial considerations are—despite the sovereign importance accorded them at the organization itself—quite subsidiary.

In 1977, a detailed study of American participation in international organizations, issued by the Senate Committee on Government Operations, considered the material circumstances of United Nations personnel in relation to the inefficiency and failures of the organization. This survey, which found pay and benefits at the United Nations astronomically higher than in the United States civil service but unrelated to ability or productivity, was disregarded. It remains a valuable record of the organization's condition during the second term of the Waldheim administration. In attributing the Secretariat's debility to the adverse effects of national interventions, the Senate committee did not trace the origins of that weakness to the actions of the United States.

6

THE ELECTION OF KURT WALDHEIM as the fourth Secretary-General of the United Nations, in December, 1971, followed the rejection by the major powers of several more substantial candidates. Of these, the Finn Max Jakobson was reportedly judged by the Soviets as incapacitated by his Jewish background for dealing with the Arab nations. Thus, while Waldheim's adult military past under Hitler was no obstacle to his appointment, Jakobson was apparently ruled out for a circumstance of his birth. (In 1986, Jakobson himself commented, "I think that was an excuse, that Moscow thought I would be too strong a Secretary-General in the tradition of Dag Hammarskjöld, and it was worried that the prestige of the office would strengthen Finland's concept of neutrality.")

Among prominent commentators, only the syndicated columnist Joseph Kraft appears to have condemned the choice, writing immediately after Waldheim's election:

> The voting was a process whereby the great powers eliminated candidates of merit. The result is a man almost certain to bring the office of Secretary-General down to the

low estate already reached by the Security Council and the General Assembly. . . .

With four strong men blocked, and the prospect of a long deadlock ahead, the hour of Ambassador Waldheim came round. Many delegates and not a few officials in the secretariat could have voiced a strong case against him . . . that he is superficial and without strong moral force; that he has done nothing of note except be pliant with all comers, beginning with the Nazis whom he served in World War II.

But what does all that signify for the great powers? Ambassador Waldheim was the preferred Russian candidate precisely because of his pliancy. The French admired his fluency in French. The British and Americans, though preferring other candidates, were not prepared to dig in for them. And the Chinese, who cast an early veto against Ambassador Waldheim, on the grounds that he was the Russian candidate, relented when Vienna gave Peking assurance of his pliancy. . . . In his first public statement after nomination by the Security Council, he emphasized that "in this position one has to know the limits."

This was, I believe, the only adverse and penetrating assessment of Waldheim's character to be published for some years. While we may wonder what Joseph Kraft had in mind when he wrote of the "strong case" that "many delegates and not a few officials in the secretariat could have voiced against him," Waldheim would, in the event, be publicly commended by his U.N. peers throughout his Secretary-Generalship and long thereafter.

Announcing Waldheim's election, the *Times* reported that "one of Mr. Waldheim's greatest assets in his successful campaign was that he was the preferred candidate of the Soviet Union from an early stage and that none of the other big powers strongly opposed him." In a subsequent article, on December 26, 1971, the *Times*—characterizing Waldheim's immediate predecessor, U Thant, as a "conciliator" and alluding to the potential activism of Jakobson—observed that "the circumstances of Mr. Waldheim's election make it pretty clear that he, too, is expected to be a conciliator." However, the *Times* conceded that the Secretary-General "has a great deal of power if he seeks it. . . . Most important, he can exercise, if he chooses, unique moral influence because unlike any other political figure in the world he is not inhibited by narrow national interests."

The anxiety of governments to "eliminate candidates of merit" in favor of this pliable one testified again to their awareness of the moral and practical potential yet remaining in the office of the Secretary-General, and in a valid and efficient international civil service. Above all, it expressed apprehension of the ultimate capacity of such a body, under vigorous leadership, to enlist the public interest in support of a more rational conduct of world affairs. The pattern of Secretariat complaisance, however, was now long established; and with Waldheim's election these governmental anxieties were set at rest.

Waldheim's efforts to secure the U.N. Secretary-Generalship had begun in the nineteen-sixties, when he served as Austria's Ambassador to the United Nations, and intensified in 1971, after he was defeated in his first bid for the Presidency of his country. His suppression of unattractive episodes from his years as a student and soldier under Hitler seems to have developed from the time of his assignment, in 1948, as First Secretary at the Austrian Legation in Paris, where the full details of his wartime experience would, if known, have aroused strong feeling. In none of his previous positions, however, had the elements of public and official scrutiny, of moral claims, and of a singular international prominence rendered the stakes so high, the risks so great, or the deception so conclusive as in the United Nations post, where the bringing to light not simply of his story but of its long concealment would have ended his public career.

In the months preceding the U.N. vote, Waldheim lobbied indefatigably for the Secretary-Generalship. Yet he knew that as a leading candidate for the position he would be investigated by the great powers and possibly by other governments; and that a variety of damaging revelations was in their hands, including a Yugoslav charge implicating him in atrocities during his suppressed wartime service in the Balkans, together with a related file in the War Crimes archive of the United Nations itself.

Waldheim evidently also knew that his candidacy would not result in exposure. How and why he obtained that assurance, and from whom, are now central questions in his ever-unfolding "case." Bureaucratic confusion, which would itself call for scrutiny and censure, cannot possibly account for a coincidence of negligence among numerous government agencies around the world in clearing a candidate of Waldheim's nationality, age, and background for so conspicuous an appointment. In recent years, investigators have speculated that Waldheim may have made some clandestine ac-

commodation with the United States authorities in the spring
of 1945, when, as he returned to Austria from the Balkans,
he was held by United States Military Intelligence for interrogation concerning the political disposition of Yugoslavia.
It is also suggested that these contacts continued in later
years. Questioned on the theme by the New York *Times* in
April, 1986, Karl Gruber, who had been Austria's Foreign
Minister in the postwar years, "did not rule out the possibility that Mr. Waldheim had some connection with American
intelligence in the years after the war. 'I don't think it probable, but one never really knows,' he said. 'It's quite possible that he did. For us, he was an Austrian official.' "

In his book *Waldheim: The Missing Years*, published in
1988, Robert E. Herzstein, a historian of the Nazi era, gives
his view that "throughout the postwar period, including his
tenure as U.N. secretary-general, Kurt Waldheim was a
U.S. intelligence asset who expected to be—and always
was—protected by his friends in the American intelligence
community." Such conjectures, which do not lack a circum-
stantial basis, are at their best attempts to explain an otherwise incomprehensible degree of official protection of Waldheim by Western governments. They cannot be dismissed
while those governments remain silent and while the United
States Department of Justice refuses to release its file on
Waldheim—despite Waldheim's own legitimate, and audacious, challenge to it to do so. Following the decision by the
United States Attorney General, in April, 1987, to place
Waldheim's name on the so-called Watch List of undesirable
aliens prohibited from entering the country, the Austrian authorities also requested that the United States make avail-

able the evidence in Waldheim's case. However, no information was provided.

For Waldheim's entry, in 1945, into his country's foreign service, on the staff of Karl Gruber, his activities under Hitler were officially reviewed. Gruber has related that he assigned this task of investigating Waldheim to his assistant, Fritz Molden, who recalls—in a "white book" entitled *Kurt Waldheim's Wartime Years: A Documentation,* prepared in Waldheim's defense by officials of the Austrian Foreign Affairs Ministry in 1987—that he, in turn, referred it first to the Ministry of the Interior and then to the United States authorities, both of which seemingly cleared Waldheim of Nazi associations. In his book *Waldheim and Austria,* Richard Bassett, a British journalist long based in Europe, notes the confused and increasingly pro-Austrian context in which such postwar "denazification" inquiries were carried on. Of the accusation lodged against Waldheim with the United Nations War Crimes Commission regarding atrocities in Yugoslavia, Bassett observes that "it is easy to see how, without conclusive evidence, Waldheim, like many others, was not subjected to too arduous an ordeal. Growing distrust of the Yugoslavs, especially after their barbaric massacring of repatriated Croats, Serbs and Slovenes in 1945, also probably contributed to a slackening of the hunt for those who may have carried out orders involving atrocities in the Balkans."

Fritz Molden, who had been, like Gruber, active in the Austrian resistance, was associated with the wartime United States Office of Strategic Services, under Allen W. Dulles. Dulles—whose daughter Molden married in 1948—helped to set up the Central Intelligence Agency in the postwar years and became its director in 1953. He was the brother of John Foster Dulles, who served as Secretary of State in the Eisenhower Administration. Karl Gruber has said that it was "probable" that Molden retained his connections with American intelligence in the years after the war.

In the course of his clearance for career employment in the new Austrian Foreign Ministry, Waldheim submitted a statement necessarily reporting not only his war service in France, Russia, and southeastern Europe but also his earlier membership in groups with Nazi associations. Robert Herzstein, who has examined the dossier containing this statement, informs us that Waldheim accounted for his enrollment in two such groups by declaring that "he could not have completed his studies without joining the Students League, nor would he have been permitted to begin his legal career without being part of some Nazi-affiliated body like the S.A. Cavalry Corps." Waldheim's application to and acceptance by the faculty of law at the University of Vienna during the years when Austria's centers of learning and her judiciary were rigorously dominated by the Nazis was in itself a strong indication of a formal connection with a Nazi organization. This reality, here referred to by Waldheim in self-extenuation, was first drawn to my attention, during Waldheim's Secretary-Generalship, by Norbert Guterman, a scholar with knowledge of the administration of European universities in the years of Nazi domination. Some attestation of adherence to Nazi doctrine would have been, as Waldheim himself now recounts, a virtual requirement for his law studies—the more so in the case of a student whose father had, as a former supporter of the Austrian reactionary Kurt von Schuschnigg, incurred Nazi displeasure at the time of the Anschluss. (As an adherent of von Schuschnigg's policy for an independent Austria, the older Waldheim was held for hours or days by the Gestapo on at least two occasions, and was dismissed from his post as a superintendent of schools.) Waldheim's repeated assertion, during his years at the United Nations, that he had remained at Vienna after 1941 pursuing his studies in the law should alone have raised immediate questions about his possible connection with the Nazi movement. While the original transgression may, according to its context, call upon our understanding, the determination to lie about these matters in afteryears, and while holding a position of claimed moral leadership, placed Waldheim squalidly and irrevocably in the wrong.

Robert Herzstein relates that in the early nineteen-fifties "the U.S. State Department solicited" from the Austrian authorities "and accepted without question a selectively edited biography of Waldheim that made it seem as if he had no military record at all." In August, 1988, in response to a renewed inquiry from the World Jewish Congress, the Central Intelligence Agency retracted a former statement that it possessed only one document concerning Kurt Waldheim, but declined to be more forthcoming. In November, 1989, however, the World Jewish Congress independently obtained a copy of a document that, referring to Waldheim's wartime service in the Balkans, is known to have been in C.I.A. records since the postwar period.

Herzstein's comment that, "for all his caution, Waldheim was nonetheless something of a gambler" is borne out by Waldheim's steady postwar quest for a prominence inexora-

63

bly paralleled by the obscuring of his early life. This aspect
of Waldheim's character is, again, most evident in his as-
siduous candidacy for the Secretary-Generalship. Whatever
assurances he may have received from informed governments that his hidden story would not be revealed, he could
not guard against its extraneous exposure by some former
comrade in arms or through the active curiosity of a scholar
or journalist outside the United Nations circle. The United
Nations archives on war criminals had been inexplicably
closed to the public since 1949; but the fact that Waldheim
was under accusation as a war criminal by the government of
Yugoslavia in the postwar years was contained in a master
list, known as the Central Registry of War Criminals and
Security Suspects, compiled by the United States Army in
1949 and publicly available in American archives since the
late nineteen-sixties. In addition to implicating Waldheim in
Nazi atrocities, the Yugoslav charge exposed Waldheim's
war service in the Balkans during the years when he claimed
to be studying in Vienna.

Following the publication, in 1986, of many concealed
facts from Waldheim's past, assertions would be made
within the bureaucracies of Austria, West Germany, and
France that senior officials of those governments had been
familiar with Waldheim's war record during his years at the
United Nations. At the time of his election as Secretary-
General, however, in December, 1971, the Western governments kept their knowledge to themselves. George Bush—
then United States Ambassador to the U.N., who in 1976
would become director of the C.I.A.—declared Waldheim
"ideally equipped" for "the duties of this high office." And

Waldheim was, as Joseph Kraft pointed out, "the preferred Russian candidate precisely because of his pliancy." The basis for Soviet confidence in Waldheim's pliancy has yet to be disclosed; but it was justified. It was to Soviet requirements that Waldheim's most conspicuous—and, on occasion, preposterous—gestures of partiality would be made, throughout his United Nations career, a fact repeatedly noted but never pursued by the press.

With hindsight, Waldheim's inaugural reference to "the limits" may be interpreted as a message to those powers who, familiar with his story, had supported his candidacy in the conviction that he must, as Secretary-General, adapt himself to their concerns. By the onset of the nineteen-seventies, however, the invocation of limits at the United Nations had become endemic and mechanical, Waldheim's words then seeming merely to echo a negativism that, at no time apologetic, would over the ensuing decade be aggressively presented as a main virtue by U.N. leaders, with the endorsement of many of their organized supporters. Similarly, the extreme operational and administrative chaos into which the organization would sink under Waldheim's stewardship was, in its first stages, scarcely distinguishable from the debility already afflicting the United Nations at the time of his election. The new Secretary-General was, indeed, greeted as a possible reformer. The London *Times* declared:

> The first place where Dr. Waldheim will have to display his talents is in the United Nations itself. The organization

65

is in bad shape. Its structure is flabby, and the morale of its staff is low. The situation cries out for an administrator who is prepared to be tough—to rationalize procedures, to promote merit and to dispense with incompetents. If this was done there would be a much better chance of producing a machine which could be called on with some confidence in a crisis.

On the last day of 1971, the New York *Times* discussed the dire condition of the organization, which was then under its recurrent threat of bankruptcy:

> The United Nations moreover has lost prestige and public support in many countries. There are those who say that a more dynamic personality could have given it the dramatic image that would have kept interest in it high.
> Mr. Thant is leaving the United Nations at a time when it is being increasingly pushed out of its basic peacekeeping function by the two superpowers, Moscow and Washington, which believe that world order must be maintained in direct negotiations by the big powers. . . . Men who have been watching the workings of the United Nations Secretariat and the relations between headquarters and the specialized agencies say that Mr. Thant's biggest failing was his "hopelessness as an administrator." Some diplomats say he lacks the toughness that it would have taken to dismiss incompetent aides. As far as is known, he never challenged a member government when it nominated an ill-equipped man to a position on the staff, one diplomat said.

When Kurt Waldheim took up his post, in January, 1972, the condition of the United Nations system was one of undisciplined expansion confusedly related to outdated concepts of global trends and inhibited at every turn by an impenetrable bureaucracy. U.N. operations, at headquarters as in the field, were beset by a lack of coherent purpose, by destructive rivalries among proliferating branches and drastic deficiencies of ability within the inflated senior ranks; and by demoralization throughout a staff body enfeebled by the almost complete absence of a merit system. Cynicism and hypocrisy on the part of governments and vested interests were compounded by an absence of salutary pressure from benevolent and academic supporters—an indulgence generally reproduced by well-intended elements of the press.

In the closing years of U Thant's tenure, the deterioration of the U.N. system had given rise to numerous internal studies, increasingly candid in content and urgent in tone, and in several instances drawn up by outside experts at the request of the U.N.'s governing bodies. From 1967 on, a series of secret reports had condemned the administration of the U.N.'s Food and Agriculture Organization, in Rome; and in 1970 a similar scrutiny of UNESCO, in Paris, brought administrative reprisals against employees who voiced support for the criticisms contained in it. (At UNESCO, in the McCarthy years, administrative violations instigated by the United States and analogous to those occurring at U.N. headquarters, in New York, had prepared the ground for this organizational chaos, which foreshadowed, in its turn, the perversion of the agency's purposes in the nineteen-seventies and -eighties.) In 1969, a massive official *Study of the Capacity of the United Nations Development System*, compiled by Sir Robert Jackson, an Australian consultant with United Nations experience, examined with unprecedented frankness the U.N.'s extensive programs of economic and social aid to underprivileged lands, and likened the enterprise to "some prehistoric monster." In the summer of 1971, a statement of causes of the demoralization of the United Nations staff was issued at Geneva by the Federation of International Civil Servants' Associations; and a lengthy article on the same theme by the respected former U.N. department head Hugh Keenleyside, appearing in the *Saturday Review*, called attention to "the tragic deterioration of the Secretariat." In October, 1971, shortly before the election of Kurt Waldheim as Secretary-General, an expert group called the Joint Inspection Unit, appointed by the General Assembly to consider aspects of the organization's predicament, released a report on personnel problems at the United Nations, in which a quarter century of administrative disarray was formidably, if incompletely, documented. Over the ensuing fifteen years, this group would continue to report on the U.N. condition.

The findings of these and of other such bodies were overwhelmingly adverse; their compilers emphatically urged immediate and radical reforms. Findings and recommendations alike would be disregarded by the organization's governmental and bureaucratic leaders; but the consequences of a willed disorder, which fatally intensified under Waldheim, had already played their part in the organization's incapacity for understanding or affecting world events.

The capital function for which the United Nations had been created—the prevention of hostilities around the world—had, from the time of Hammarskjöld's death, in

September, 1961, lapsed as an active concept at the U.N., replaced by a claim that the organization's usefulness lay in providing a place for national envoys to forgather, and a forum for face-saving rhetoric in the wake of decisions taken elsewhere. The public, however, could not necessarily assume that the leaders of modern nations would find no means of meeting or expressing themselves, when they wished to do so, without the baroque apparatus of the present United Nations; and possibly doubted (since the crucial gestures of great power were consistently made outside the United Nations) the U.N.'s assertion that the organization had by its mere existence been instrumental in averting nuclear conflict—a claim, quite unsupported by facts, that could only be conclusively disproved by the cataclysm itself. During the nineteen-sixties, this profound change—essentially a conversion to passivity—in the organization's declared idea of its political purposes was accomplished almost uncontested. In the same period, the definition of U.N. "peace-keeping" dwindled from its previous concept of creative intervention, coming to signify, as it does today, not the establishment of peace but, rather, at best, a suspension of long and unresolved hostilities, in which the United Nations and its troops might supervise a plebiscite or a precarious truce. This was a falling off from Hammarskjöld's sustained attempt to address the sources of conflict; and to forestall war, with all its attendant ruin.

For most of U Thant's tenure, from 1961 to 1972, the world's attention had been fixed on the last excruciating stage of the thirty years' conflict in Indo-China—the Vietnam War, which the United Nations never seriously considered. The Secretary-General's obscure attempts at mediation of that war had proved ineffectual, and his personal aversion to the conflict—voiced, at the time, only in rare and unremarkable asides—provided no leadership, support, or stature for the worldwide call for its termination; or for a growing element of popular rejection, within the world's more stable societies, of the phenomenon of war—a rejection in which the United Nations had its origins. The pattern of U.N. impotence in all emergencies directly involving the superpowers had been emphasized by the peripheral and ritualistic role assigned to the United Nations during the Cuban missile crisis of October, 1962—when, before the world, the heads of the two great opposing forces contested the issue, and, between them, allayed the danger; and in August, 1968, when the representatives of Czechoslovakia fruitlessly appealed, as had their Hungarian counterparts in 1956, to the United Nations against Soviet repression. The weakness of the United Nations' performance in hostilities between India and Pakistan in 1965, and, in the early nineteen-seventies in the prolonged emergency of the new state of Bangladesh, had exposed unresponsiveness in the Secretariat as well as in the U.N.'s political organs. U.N. aloofness from the fratricidal struggle between Nigeria and Biafra, which would cost at least a million lives, prefigured the organization's disengagement from analogous tragedies that would overwhelm Uganda, Burundi, and other African states in the coming decade; and vitiated, with its pall of selective morality, the strength of U.N. pronouncements regarding apartheid in South Africa.

The Secretariat's own lack of standing and influence in

these events, its failure to rally the energies of those governments willing to act responsibly, and its insistence on its subjection not only to governmental desires but to their lowest common denominator were absorbed into the public mind with a lingering sediment of disdain. In that context, U Thant's 1967 removal of U.N. forces from the Sinai shortly before the outbreak of the Six-Day War appeared—whatever the disclaimers of United Nations spokesmen—to confirm the image of an irresolute institution under an inept and timorous leader.

7

THE VERY DANGERS of world conditions, and growing public apprehension of a wave of violence and disaffection around the earth offered, in 1972, great opportunities to a new Secretary-General. Many thoughtful citizens were disposed, in their anxiety, to consider remedies of an international and humanitarian character. The war in Asia had impaired America's ability to speak for democratic principle, as she had done since the close of the Second World War. At the United Nations itself, the admission of mainland China to membership, after a twenty-year exclusion at the behest of the United States, signalled—together with the entry of newly independent nations—a modification of American hegemony. The economic might of the United States, with its contingent powers of political compulsion, was, furthermore, no longer unrivalled around the world. An outbreak of authoritarianism had given rise to fresh concern for human and civil rights on the part of groups and individuals in many lands; and the emergence of voluntary agencies protesting, with wide public support, the official practice of torture and unlawful imprisonment threw into relief the United Nations' long abdication from its duties in that field, and its adherence to procedures cruelly and blatantly favoring offending governments. Dissidents—their very names unmentionable in United Nations assemblies—fearlessly coming forward with their testimony in the Soviet Union, Asia, Africa, and Latin America, recalled to the public imagination the power of individual moral courage and endurance, and of articulate truth. All these mutations presented an occasion for loosening the bonds of Secretariat servitude to governments, in favor of a new involvement with responsible elements of the public. Within the Secretariat, also, the severe debility reported by the United Nations' own surveys gave a mandate for radical reform.

Kurt Waldheim had not been chosen in order to seize such an opportunity; nor had any of his predecessors in office, although one had—as is recorded—surprised his sponsors. In Waldheim's case, those secret constraints imposed by his concealed past were necessary only to give form to a failure that his character already insured. Uninspired, officious, and essentially trivial, Waldheim was proof against every occasion of a larger kind. A lack of imagination, which indubitably sustained him in his long deception, precluded any sense of self-absurdity. The satisfaction in "limits" expressed at the time of his appointment extended to his own shortcomings; and, as he took office, he informed the world, "I'm glad I'm not an intellectual ball of fire. I don't think you can solve the United Nations' problems that way."

An antipathy to distinguished thought and to individual powers of reason and discernment had played a prominent role in the purges of the Secretariat conducted under Trygve

Lie—and had been indeed a cornerstone of the McCarthyist movement in the United States. In 1953, Henri Hoppenot, the representative of France, had deplored to the General Assembly "a mediocre level of recruitment" at the Secretariat, which had "left deep marks on the administrative habits of the organization." In 1974, in a study highly critical of United Nations recruitment and administrative practices prepared by Seymour Maxwell Finger and John Mugno, of the Ralph Bunche Institute of the City University of New York, U.N. administrators themselves agreed, if anonymously, that the organization has "never hired the cream of the crop," and "has settled perhaps too easily for average quality personnel." This study, which angered Waldheim by its criticisms of his overriding desire to gratify governmental pressures, also noted the unflagging determination of member states to perpetuate the weak condition of an international service that in fact presented, by now, no significant challenge to immediate national interests:

> Although the Secretary-General and the Secretariat have been less bold since Hammarskjöld's death, representation in the Secretariat, and especially at its highest posts, is still seen by many states as insurance against unwanted Secretariat action on political, economic or social issues, or as an opportunity to prompt the Secretariat to enunciate a particular position on these issues.

United Nations leaders, were, however, unmoved by such reflections, which came only briefly, if at all, to public attention. And soon after the release of this particular study a "restructuring" of U.N. economic and social operations, announced in May, 1975, inaugurated an unprecedented increase of new senior posts assigned for geographical distribution. This innovation was hailed by Kurt Waldheim as "historic."

In the senior circle of the organization, where the prodigy of Hammarskjöld's term had left no legacy, innate limitations provided, in the new year of 1972, a comfortable ambience for Waldheim, as did the larger institutional context of conformity and fear. "The freedom of the mind, the source of every generous and rational sentiment"—in Gibbon's words—"was destroyed by the habits of credulity and submission." Processes of national screening and the compilation of secret United Nations dossiers had, together with other forms of intimidation and reprisal, now been at work on U.N. personnel for a quarter-century, in violation of the Charter—and it is perfectly indicative of the U.N. paradox that tens of thousands of useless and defamatory files should have been maintained by the administration as a weapon against its staff while throughout the nineteen-seventies the Secretary-General's own history lay unconsulted in public records and in the War Crimes archive of the United Nations itself. (More striking still is the fact that the machinery of "clearance," established by governments to sift and expose eccentricities in the staff body, should have shown itself entirely and willfully ineffectual in the case of the organization's leader.) The Secretariat had clogged its upper and intermediate ranks with bureaucrats and politicians transplanted or on loan from national administrations, at the expense of independent candidates who had breathed the free air of private life, and who would have refreshed the institution with diversity and a sense of proportion. The almost complete absence of competitive examinations or other objective standards reflected the fact that admission to and advancement within the international civil service were controlled by improper extraneous factors. In 1971, the Joint Inspection Unit had recorded the "remarkable fact that a very large number of Professional staff have never attended a university," adding that in this senior category of the Secretariat "more than 25 per cent seem never to have attended an establishment of higher education."

The clear provisions of the United Nations Charter for the creation of a rational and distinguished career service had been, with the Secretariat's complicity, completely set aside. The international civil service, as a coherent entity, had never come into being. Nor, under its prevailing leadership, could it do so.

8

ALTHOUGH IN BECOMING the fourth Secretary-General of the United Nations, in January, 1972, Kurt Waldheim assumed control of an enfeebled organization, an assessment of the United Nations' deterioration under his leadership is no mere study of degrees of incapacity. Waldheim's appeasement of member governments—which was eager and obsessive, in contrast to the wan docility of his immediate predecessor, U Thant—occurred within a world whose mounting disorder arose, increasingly, from popular, parochial, or anarchistic movements before whose insistence or fanaticism governments themselves were in many cases helpless. The long preoccupation of Secretariat officials with governmental contacts, and their awe of established position, had not only left them without prescience and influence in this larger sphere but encouraged their inaccessibility to the public concern, and an unreality toward those events, ideas, and transfigurations that did not come before the United Nations. Legalistic deliberations at the U.N. on crises with which the world was urgently seized were greeted by the organization as initiatives; while, to the public, they merely emphasized the

U.N.'s self-indulgence and its removal from the pace and nature of new realities. Waldheim's tenure was to be dense with irreproachable statements on global peril, and punctuated by referrals of critical questions to governmental bodies whose inaction was assured—these exercises being treasured up by commentators on United Nations affairs as evidence of the Secretary-General's "independence and activism." In 1972, the first year of his incumbency, Waldheim called on the General Assembly to discuss the question of terrorism. (In December, 1985, having considered the matter for thirteen years, the Assembly agreed—as the New York *Times* reported—to the adoption of "a landmark resolution . . . that condemns all acts of terrorism as 'criminal.' ") In 1973, the *Times* noted that a U.N. body "has been trying to find a definition for the word 'aggression' for 23 years. . . . As a result of this stagnation the major powers deal with each other directly in all important aspects of their relationships." The *Times* article concluded, however, by endorsing a favored U.N. view: "In the words of Charles Yost . . . a former representative here, 'just existing is perhaps the most important quality of the United Nations.' "

Waldheim's own attitude toward his responsibilities was quoted by the *Times*, in connection with the issue of terrorism, on December 20, 1972: "Once the item was inscribed and the Assembly agreed to consider the matter, I had done my job. The rest was up to the 132 member nations." Meanwhile, the "real world" pursued its ways and its wars. On that same day, a *Times* editorial on the Vietnam War—a conflict virtually undiscussed by the United Nations—cited the proposal of a United States Air Force general that North Vietnam "be bombed back to the Stone Age."

It is to Brian Urquhart—as Waldheim's Under Secretary-General for Special Political Affairs, and a leading United Nations spokesman for the Waldheim years—that we must continually turn for the organization's own conception of its performance during that decade of the nineteen-seventies. Although in his autobiography, published in 1987, Urquhart criticizes Waldheim's tendency to be "too accessible to the media," Urquhart's own role in that respect appears more prominent—his public addresses, interviews, and interventions representing, together with his published views on U.N. matters, a large commitment of professional time. (Bernard Nossiter, who was chief U.N. correspondent of the *Times* in the latter years of the Waldheim era, has admiringly confirmed, in a review of Urquhart's memoirs, that "seasoned reporters and diplomats . . . would march past the secretary-general's office" in order to obtain Urquhart's views.) Urquhart, in his many public pronouncements, evidently shared the official estimate of Waldheim as a vigorous leader chafing at governmental restraints. Commenting in 1981, in *Foreign Affairs,* on the apparent ineffectuality of the Security Council, he felt that "Secretary-General Waldheim has made persistent efforts to provide leadership and initiative in successive crises." Such a judgment of Waldheim, as a thwarted activist, was by then unlikely to find an echo in public opinion, formed in the manifest realities of Waldheim's conduct and character, and of United Nations inadequacy, during ten years of drastic world events.

In the field of human rights, the apostasy of U.N. bodies appointed to deplore and prevent governmental persecutions had, in closing and perverting a legitimate outlet for the grievance of undefended victims, already contributed to violence around the world.

In 1968, as persecutions in Iran under the Pahlavis became a preoccupation in the West, an International Conference on Human Rights opened in Teheran, sponsored and inaugurated by the Shah. U Thant, in an opening address, found it "very fitting" that the twentieth anniversary of the adoption of the United Nations Universal Declaration of Human Rights should be thus commemorated in Iran. In 1970, the Shah's sister, Princess Ashraf, was elected by acclamation to the chair of the United Nations Commission on Human Rights. The Shah's elimination of moderate political elements in Iran would itself contribute to the later ascendancy of extremism in that country. United Nations complaisance toward the Shah was to be a principal factor—acknowledged, in January, 1980, by Waldheim himself to ABC News as he returned from a futile journey to Teheran—in the Secretary-General's inability to negotiate with the Khomeini regime for the release of United States hostages.

As Waldheim began his decade at the U.N., he had asserted to the General Assembly that the "unwritten moral responsibility which every Secretary-General bears does not allow him to turn a blind eye when innocent civilian lives are placed in jeopardy on a large scale." By 1974, however, Amnesty International had presented, to U.N. humanitarian organs, innumerable cases of official torture and unlawful imprisonment in diverse lands; and had obtained little response. During a brief and excruciating session early in 1974, the U.N. Commission on Human Rights agreed sub rosa to play down torture in Chile in exchange for silence on Soviet dissidents. Under pressure from independent humanitarian groups and from world opinion, the Commission would subsequently investigate and censure Chilean violations. (On December 4, 1972, at the United Nations General Assembly, President Salvador Allende of Chile had appealed in vain against actions—by United States governmental, industrial, and banking interests, and by the World Bank itself— intended to bring his government down. Following this fruitless plea, Allende returned to Chile, where he met his death.) In 1974, the permanent transfer of the Human Rights Commission from New York to Geneva was widely attributed to a desire to reduce public scrutiny. Through the Commission's procedures, the confidential appeals of dissidents on occasion found their way back to the offending governments—the United Nations thus delivering victims into the hands of their oppressors. (In May, 1979, *Newsweek* stated—in an article regarding a concentration in Geneva of senior U.N. officials identified as K.G.B. agents—that "at the U.N.'s human-rights division, the names of Soviet dissidents who write to protest about repression are sent to appropriate authorities in Moscow by 'senior human-rights officer' Yuri Reshetov.") Commenting, in May, 1977, on the Commission's disregard of mass atrocities committed under Idi Amin in Uganda, the *Times* of London stated in an editorial:

This was a repetition of United Nations indifference to the massacres, not less horrible or numerous, though less publicised, which occurred in Burundi. (Indeed, United

81

Nations agencies in Burundi were accused of cooperating with President Micombero.) . . .

In short, the Human Rights Commission has little or nothing to do with rights, justice or human conscience. It is, or has become, a political and propaganda body. It makes a mockery of human rights, as solemnly written into international conventions.

Persecutions in Greece, India, Indonesia, and the Philippines, in Central and South America, and in all territories under Soviet control were similarly ignored or evaded by U.N. bodies during the nineteen-seventies. In 1974, the Secretary-General's official spokesman espoused a view already current in U.N. circles, that "Western" concepts of rights should not necessarily be urged on other cultures—although it is presumably of such standards that the United Nations Universal Declaration of Human Rights is composed. A published assertion by the U.N. Secretariat itself that the Universal Declaration "does not have the force of law" was publicly deplored, in 1977, by a retired director of the U.N. Division of Human Rights. This inconsistency even of stating, let alone applying, its decreed principles of human rights had infected the organization from its earliest years. Speaking, in 1957, of the "many cases where the United Nations have failed," Winston Churchill pointed out, "Justice cannot be a hit-or-miss system. We cannot be content with an arrangement where our new system of international laws applies only to those who are willing to keep them."

Brian Urquhart, who in 1982 felt that, in regard to human rights, "we have not done very well on that in my view so far. I have no doubt we shall do better in the future," praised the organization in 1986 for "the putting of human rights onto an international level that governments can't ignore anymore, which is a fantastic achievement in my view." To a student of the human-rights record of the United Nations this praise is astonishing.

Years of resistance by governments to the creation of a post of United Nations High Commissioner for Human Rights had further weakened the organization's scant credit in this field, where the propitiating of evil by United Nations leaders themselves presents one of the most melancholy spectacles of the United Nations story. Theo van Boven, of the Netherlands, who assumed, in 1977, the existing position of director, approached his duties with objectivity and conscience. The termination of van Boven's U.N. service, early in 1982, was one of the first consequences of the election of the new Secretary-General, Javier Pérez de Cuéllar, of Peru. On February 11th of that year, the New York *Times* reported, from Geneva, van Boven's statement that "he was leaving the post because of 'major policy differences with the leadership of the organization in New York,' " and went on to say:

He declined to comment when questioned by reporters about reports that his five-year appointment, which expires at the end of April, was not being renewed by Secretary-General Javier Pérez de Cuéllar because of opposition from Latin American governments.

In a speech at the beginning of the current session [of the U.N. Commission on Human Rights], Mr. van Boven had mentioned reports of political murders in Chile, El Salvador and Guatemala as he called on the commission to take "appropriate and meaningful action" against the "taking of human lives by organized power."

In his remarks to the commission today, Mr. van Boven said he had "always felt that our primary duty is toward the peoples in whose name the United Nations Charter was written. I have also maintained," he continued, "that whenever necessary we must speak out on matters of principle, regardless of whom we please or displease within or outside the organization."

Acting upon such convictions, van Boven could not remain in the United Nations' service.

On January 30, 1989, as the U.N. Commission on Human Rights began its annual six-week session at Geneva, the *Times* of London observed in an editorial, "The Commission's lacklustre performance over the years in bringing governments, the principal offenders, to book has done much to damage the U.N.'s standing with the public." In March, the session concluded with a perfunctory measure designed to avoid the issue of rights violations in Cuba, the New York *Times* reporting that "when the vote was announced, the Cuban delegates cheered, threw papers in the air and leaped over desks to embrace their third world supporters." In August, 1989, a United Nations human-rights assembly directly criticized, for the first time, abuses by one of the five permanent members of the Security Council—a subsidiary body of the Human Rights Commission voting by secret ballot to place the issue of rights violations in China before a meeting of the full Commission in 1990, as a matter of concern. To have passed over the Chinese brutalities so recently witnessed by the world would have shown the Commission utterly recreant. Its action, moderate enough, exacerbated a movement, led—at the subsequent General Assembly— by China and supported by Third World representatives, to render the U.N. virtually inactive in the cause of human rights.

In other international humanitarian efforts, United Nations relief undertakings—greatly expanded in the nineteen-seventies, as the victims of prolonged conflicts and natural disasters multiplied—were gratuitously obstructed by the U.N. pattern of subservience to governmental pressures, of administrative havoc, and of feuds nurtured within U.N. agencies themselves. While the public was encouraged to regard the existence of a United Nations relief mission as a concerted endeavor by the organization, devoted workers in the field were repeatedly frustrated in essential tasks by the confusion and politicization of a top-heavy headquarters bureaucracy. Nothing in the United Nations' attitudes and structure had prepared the system to respond with coördinated intelligence to an unprecedented volume of calamities—which were associated, in Asia, with the dispersal of entire peoples and societies. Nor were correctives rationally applied: UNDRO, a U.N. agency for disaster-relief coördination created in 1971 to remedy the disorder of U.N. operations, was discovered only in 1980, by a U.N. expert group known as the Joint Inspection Unit, merely to have provided sinecures for appointees who rarely visited a disaster site.

Of the U.N.'s response—in its relief operation in Bangladesh—to one of the first such large challenges, Brian Urquhart has written with unqualified enthusiasm. In 1978, in his foreword to *The United Nations in Bangladesh*—a book by Thomas W. Oliver, who had worked with the U.N. relief enterprise—Urquhart stated, "The operation was a happy combination of multilateral and bilateral effort concerted by the United Nations. It was also an example of the whole U.N. system working as a team and speaking with one voice." This assessment—echoed by Oliver near the conclusion of his study, but by no means borne out in the text of his account itself—is in contrast to the appraisal of the United Nations' performance in that prolonged emergency compiled in a confidential report by Toni Hagen. Hagen served, from late 1971 into the spring of 1972, as chief of the U.N. relief mission during the period of political convulsion and natural catastrophe that attended the birth of the nation of Bangladesh. His report—transmitted, as it were, from the battlefield—reflects the severance, familiar to many who have served on U.N. missions, of field workers from an unresponsive and unrealistic head office. Hagen repeatedly appeals against "a total lack of organization at headquarters and the deaf ear of New York *vis-à-vis* the people in the field," contrasts the arrangements of private relief agencies favorably with those of the United Nations, and deplores the headquarters' performance as "one single chain of disregard and nonacceptance of advice from the field." Thomas Oliver, who describes Hagen as "a Swiss geologist of some distinction" (Hagen had in fact served the United Nations for many years as one of its ablest field experts), criticizes his "unorthodox, outspoken" manner and charges him with misjudgment; but acknowledges that Hagen, "vigorous and experienced in relief work," was "well liked by his staff, most of whom believed, and continue to believe, that he was the right man for the job at that stage in the operation." Hagen's two-volume report is not specifically cited among Oliver's sources; nor is it clear whether Oliver is aware of that document's existence. The episode illustrates an insurmountable difficulty, for the public, in arriving at informed judgments of United Nations undertakings. An official statement that praises a U.N. operation as exemplary, and gives no indication of the fundamental recorded dissent of a leading field officer supported by the majority of his staff, can scarcely be challenged by citizens having no knowledge of crucial sources of disagreement. As a result of his experience in Bangladesh, Hagen withdrew from United Nations service. His forthright criticism would in any case have made his continued presence intolerable to the Secretariat leadership.

Defects adversely affecting international relief have been drawn to public attention in independent accounts such as William Shawcross's *The Quality of Mercy* (1984), Dan Jacobs's *The Brutality of Nations* (1987), Graham Hancock's *Lords of Poverty* (1989), and the article "Famine," by Raymond Bonner, published in *The New Yorker* on March 13, 1989. An earlier study critical of the United Nations' performance in large-scale relief operations—*The Politics of Starvation*, by Jack Shepherd—was issued by the Carnegie Endowment for International Peace in 1975.

In addition to relief work, many worthy ventures would be launched, in the nineteen-seventies, by the proliferating agencies of the United Nations. But their effectiveness was consistently inhibited by the stranglehold of a politicized central authority and its administrative disarray—essential undertakings often depending for their usefulness on the extent to which able persons in the field could outmaneuver or disregard their head office. The tribulations of mission personnel—or, on occasion, of an entire staff body—seeking to prevail over the deficiencies or improprieties of their leadership have been a constant of United Nations service, acutely illustrated in the early years under Trygve Lie, and subsequently during the Waldheim decade. Outsiders, including myself, who have appealed against such conditions can testify to the imperviousness of Secretariat officials—an inaccessibility supported by a costly official apparatus of public information and propaganda. The unequal struggle between integrity and unfitness, carried on for decades and debilitating to every United Nations action, comes to public attention only rarely and in its most emphatic forms. In 1979, a leading United Nations representative in Cyprus was recalled and censured for extensive thefts of Cypriot antiquities only after local police raided his home—the New York *Times* reporting that "the issue of missing treasures has been raised many times with United Nations officials by the Government, which asked for their help to prevent them being taken out of the country." Ten years later, in 1989, the U.N. High Commissioner for Refugees withdrew from his post only after charges of misconduct, and of the profound demoralization of his staff, were prominently reported in the press. The underlying condition remains endemic, inexcusable, and unaddressed.

9

IN KURT WALDHEIM'S first months at the United Nations, it was evident that he would offer no leadership whatever toward resolving the Secretariat's subjection to governmental interests. In July, 1972, his appeal for protection of the dikes in North Vietnam was contemptuously dismissed by President Nixon; and Waldheim did not further provoke the great powers. (Following the October War, of 1973, between Egypt and Israel, Waldheim expressed his gratitude that the United Nations had been called in to complement the joint conciliatory effort undertaken by Henry Kissinger, of the United States, and Soviet leaders.)

Early in Waldheim's tenure, there were indications that his extreme receptivity to national pressures possibly originated—as in the case of the first Secretary-General, Trygve Lie—in compulsions beyond the acknowledged sphere of U.N. weakness.

The United Nations had never concerned itself with violations of human rights occurring under Soviet jurisdiction; and would not do so, even tangentially, for years. Throughout Waldheim's U.N. decade, however, disclosures regarding the vast prison network of the Soviet Union continued to be made, within and outside Russia, by intrepid survivors. These revelations, which transfixed the world's attention, were ignored only in the councils and human-rights bodies of the United Nations, and at the Secretariat itself. Such primary failures were merged in the more general abdication by U.N. organs—an abdication obscured, in its turn, by lack of public expectations. In 1974, however, Secretariat leaders became discernibly more active in an effort to gratify totalitarian power. In February of that year, Vittorio Winspeare Guicciardi, the director-general of the United Nations office in Geneva, acting at the instigation of the Soviet government, caused a work of Aleksandr Solzhenitsyn to be removed from commercial shops on the U.N.'s Geneva premises, in the Palais des Nations. Solzhenitsyn's *The Gulag Archipelago* had recently been published, in Russian, in Paris, and had made its appearance in the bookshops of the West—an event that would precipitate, in that same month of February, the author's arrest by the Soviet police and his deportation into exile.

Under the United Nations Charter, the organization's international personnel are sworn not to "seek or receive instructions from any government"; in accordance with the U.N. Universal Declaration of Human Rights, they are bound to uphold the free circulation of ideas and information "through any media and regardless of frontiers." Censorship of Solzhenitsyn by the United Nations drew protests in the European press, and from two hundred and fifty of the several thousand U.N. employees in Geneva. Persisting into July, the affair aroused questions during a press conference at Geneva conducted jointly by Waldheim and Winspeare Guicciardi. To these inquiries, Waldheim responded by asserting his dedication to "the long standing principle of freedom of information," without accounting for the removal, by stealth, from commercial shops, of a work being read around the world. His subordinate spoke of his "obligation," and that of the booksellers themselves, to avoid giving displeasure to "certain delegates" by the display of a publication "*à caractère outrageant pour un État Membre.*" Following this remarkable press conference, the U.N.'s action was prominently protested by PEN and in the *Times Book Review*; and the book was, at least for a time, restored to the Geneva shelves.

Waldheim's acquiescence in the Soviet demand for removal of Solzhenitsyn's work, and his adherence for months to a highly exposed act of political censorship, invite the suspicion that he acted out of fear. His conduct here belongs to the same aberrant category as his order, as Foreign Minister of Austria in 1968, for the rejection of numbers of Czech refugees attempting to enter Austria after the Soviet invasion of Czechoslovakia. (That order was disobeyed by the Austrian Ambassador at Prague, Rudolf Kirchschläger, against whom no disciplinary action was taken.) It is of a piece with his refusal, in April, 1975, to issue even so much as an appeal to Communist leaders in Vietnam on behalf of refugees; and with his notable condemnation—as "a serious violation of the national sovereignty of a United Nations member state"—of the 1976 rescue by Israeli commandos of Israeli hostages from Entebbe airport in Uganda. These and numerous other actions and pronouncements lend their peculiar evidence to the larger trends suggested by Waldheim's apparent endorsement, at a conference on Indo-Chinese refugees in July, 1979, of Vietnam's intention to stem what Waldheim called "illegal" departures from Vietnamese territory; by his reluctance to convene a conference of settlement following Vietnam's invasion of Cambodia; or by his prompt and manifest espousal, in the mid-nineteen-seventies, of the shift throughout U.N. bodies toward condemnation of Israel on the part of the Arab nations. Of Waldheim's tepid response to conciliatory moves between Egypt and Israel, the New York *Times* reported, in February, 1978, that "he showed hesitancy about supporting the Egyptian-Israeli peace initiative, apparently because of disapproval by the Soviet Union, Syria, and more extremist Arabs." Possibilities of long-term reconciliation were thus sacrificed, by the United Nations Secretary-General, to the immediate requirements of hostile factions.

In June, 1986, in its first reference to those revelations of Waldheim's past published months earlier in the West, the Soviet press vehemently defended Waldheim as having played "an active role" in the passage of U.N. resolutions dealing with "Israel's aggression against Arab countries." Soviet fidelity to Waldheim, who served with the German Army on the Russian front in 1941 and near sites of Nazi atrocities in southeastern Europe in later years, is no more readily comprehensible than Soviet support of his original candidacy for the Secretary-Generalship—unless we may read explicit meaning into Joseph Kraft's 1971 observation that "Waldheim was the preferred Russian candidate precisely because of his pliancy."

In 1977, following his reëlection, with Soviet and United States support, to a second term as Secretary-General, Waldheim, in Moscow, presented the Soviet leader, Leonid Brezhnev, with a United Nations peace medal "in recognition of his considerable and fruitful activities in favor of universal peace and people's security." In return, according to the *Times* of London, which carried a photograph of the ceremony, "Mr. Brezhnev gave Dr. Waldheim a collection of medals from different Soviet republics"—Brezhnev thus contributing to a remarkable set of decorations that included Waldheim's medals from the Russian front itself, as well as from his wartime exploits in the Balkans. The accompanying talks were described by Tass as "extremely cordial." This event took place as political, intellectual, and ethnic persecutions by Soviet authorities were the focus of worldwide protest and of individual challenge within Russia itself. Whatever the intentions of those who expunged, in 1952, from the U.N. staff regulations, the General Assembly prohibition against employment at the United Nations of persons discreditably associated with Nazism and Fascism, they can hardly have included the possibility that such a figure would within twenty years become Secretary-General of the organization, decorated and commended by the leader of the Soviet Union.

Since 1977, Soviet policies have greatly altered, and it seems unlikely that the nation's younger leaders will continue to adhere to Waldheim's cause. Should they discover, as Soviet change continues, an ultimate advantage in disclosing the basis of Waldheim's relations with their predecessors, we may obtain the key to the entire Waldheim enigma.

At the United Nations, Waldheim's former colleagues have asserted that his favors were evenly distributed, showing no bias toward the Soviet Union. Aside from Waldheim's mani-

fest accommodation of Soviet requirements, we need only re-
call his disparagement, in 1975, of Western condemnation of
his refusal to appeal on behalf of Vietnamese refugees—"The
criticism comes from the West exclusively. . . . The rest of
the world seems satisfied"—to feel the unreality of these
judgments: an analogous dismissal, on Waldheim's part, of
the views of the Soviet bloc would have been inconceivable.
The favors prominently, and outrageously, extended by
Waldheim to Soviet interests during his U.N. years raise the
question of what further services he may have covertly per-
formed. In the spring of 1986, the Western press carried reports from Yugoslav sources that documents concerning
Waldheim had been relayed by a Yugoslav intelligence agent
to his Soviet counterpart, in the immediate postwar period.
The double agent Arkady Shevchenko, who before his defec-
tion to Washington was a member of Waldheim's U.N. Cabi-
net, agreed that Waldheim's Balkan history was probably in
Soviet hands; but dismissed the likelihood that the material
was used to blackmail the Secretary-General, since Shevchenko himself was never employed by Moscow to that end,
and "I would have been the logical person to do it." Shevchenko's word is presumably no more reliable than Waldheim's. And Moscow, surveying the pair of them, may have
felt that—in the words of George Eliot—"to act with double-
ness towards a man whose own conduct was double, was so
near an approach to virtue that it deserved to be called by no
meaner name than diplomacy."

10

AN OPPORTUNITY NOT SEIZED is an elusive theme for speculation, and one the public finds difficult to address. During
Kurt Waldheim's decade at the United Nations, a rising public perception of the unfitness of the organization, and of its
Secretary-General, was belligerently repudiated by U.N.
leaders who, praising Waldheim's conduct of his office,
defended as a positive factor his appeasement of national
pressures, evidently without pondering the possible root, or
effect, of such servitude. In September, 1981, as the Waldheim era at the U.N. drew to its close in a world beset by new
conflict, Brian Urquhart, as the Secretary-General's senior
deputy and chief spokesman, applauded what he considered
Waldheim's achievement: "In terms of usefulness, not glamor, he's actually been the best Secretary-General. He's
done what none of the others did, kept on working terms with
almost everyone, which is essential. He also manages to get
people together in a reasonably constructive spirit and helps
them find areas of agreement. People are always underrating
him." There was, at that period, little in the context of world

affairs to suggest that such tactics of appeasement on Waldheim's part were proving efficacious.

For Urquhart, Waldheim was, in a favorite characterization, "an honest broker." Yet this metaphor—given currency
by Bismarck—seems out of place: honesty was at no time
conspicuous in Waldheim, and his relations with the world's
powers were never those of a disinterested mediator.

Unchallenged by the media, flattered in their immediate
circle, the senior officials of the Secretariat had become ac-
customed to telling rather than listening, and to treating public concern not as a power to be mobilized but as an imperti-
nence, and as still another phenomenon to be countered. The
silencing of inquiry—even when it touched the very matters
censured in the U.N.'s internal reports, or raised issues of
fundamental principle—with peremptory rebuke or arcane
statutory excuse played its extended role in alienating the
public, and in blunting the organization's long-reduced appetite for self-comprehension. "I think that there is now a great
fashion for slamming the U.N. whether it is merited or not,"
Brian Urquhart told a television audience in 1982. Valid objections—lumped together, as in this instance, with ground-
less ones, as "slamming" or "bashing"—were thus dismissed
as the pursuit of a "great fashion." Because, at its inception,
the United Nations had been a target of reactionaries and
opportunists—against whom no U.N. leader had raised his
voice—every subsequent critic would be characterized as
isolationist or self-seeking. By now, however, the capital
source of public misgiving toward the United Nations lay in
the organization's own mismanagement and improvidence,
and in its moral and intellectual failure before the world. In

their refusal to take the meaning of public doubts, which were often an expression of residual interest in U.N. potential, United Nations officials stigmatized criticism without weighing it, and evaded, year after year, its legitimate content. The international enterprise was, in this way, denied all opportunity for reassessment and renewal.

In an interview in the New York *Times Magazine* of December 19, 1982, Urquhart stated his belief, inculcated by experiences in the Second World War, that "the worst way to make an argument is by reason and good information. You must appeal to people's emotions and to their fears of being made to look ridiculous." Not everyone will agree that reason is the worst foundation for advancing opinions, or prove a willing subject for such tactics. Urquhart's basic tenets for peacekeeping—enumerated by the *Times* at his retirement, in 1986—are all prohibitions, each introduced by the word "Don't." The depreciation of reason reiterated in that list, together with drastic figures of speech—"Don't dive into an empty pool," "Don't ask people you are dealing with to commit suicide"—illuminates the Secretariat mood.

While, in the Waldheim years, circumscription and negation were urged on the public as the organization's chief qualities, the supreme asset of the Secretary-General's office—moral example—was repeatedly devalued by the incumbent himself. "All I have is moral power. I have nothing behind me," Waldheim said, at a press conference reported by the *Times* of London, in 1977. "I can write letters to people. I can speak personally to governments, but I have not got the power to force anyone to do anything." Of this despondent assessment, the newspaper observed that "Dr. Waldheim

gave the impression of a man resigned to being the spokesman for the largest body in the world equipped with the least
number of teeth." Here, and in his writings, Waldheim
speaks incidentally of moral power, as if it were a current of
low wattage to be switched on at will. Moral distinction as an
inward quality, arduously earned, and unvaunted, eludes
him even as a concept, let alone as an attainment capable of
moving nations.

Urquhart's own endorsement of Waldheim, as expressed to
the press and in his respective prefaces to English-language
editions of two books by Waldheim, seems equivocal on this
paramount issue of Waldheim's moral stature. "Men like Urquhart call Waldheim courageous as well as decent," the
Washington *Post* reported in January, 1980, going on to
quote Urquhart's view that "the Secretary-General is the honest broker in the game of world politics and he really has to
tailor his conduct to that world. He has to quiet their fears,
angers, listen to 152 nations. He really has to see all sides. It
doesn't appear to be a very heroic stance very often—and
shouldn't, if you're going to do it right." Although it is difficult to see how, in that context, moral leadership can be created at all, articles by the organization's advocates appearing
in the American and British press in the immediate post-
Waldheim years continue to strike the same note: "Waffle,
but Still Worthwhile," by Sir Anthony Parsons, in the London
Times of October 6, 1984, and "When Nothing Is Better than
Nothing," by Conor Cruise O'Brien, in the same newspaper
on October 23, 1985, are examples—the one abject, the
other bombastic—of the irrationality to which United Nations
apologists have been carried by their compulsion to vindicate

the organization's passivity. Sir Anthony, a genial British representative at the United Nations in the late Waldheim years, concedes that "to the uninitiated" the "stupefying boredom" of U.N. proceedings "may well appear to be a grievous waste of time, money and effort"; but continues to hope, of U.N. encounters, that "this kind of thing must have some value." O'Brien, for his part, takes to task any lingering diehards who might ask "Why did the United Nations not do something to prevent those wars" in which "twenty million people are estimated to have died . . . since 1945?" O'Brien asserts, "The question is misconceived. The United Nations cannot do anything, and never could"—before proceeding to his contention that the U.N.'s value to its members "is its proven capacity to fail, and to be seen to fail." Of these U.N. failures—staged, according to O'Brien, to allow governments to modify an aggressive stance—he observes, "Shoddy, but probably preferable to the honest, brave courses whose rejection the United Nations theatre facilitated by obscuring." A later article by O'Brien, in the *Times Literary Supplement* of November 6–12, 1987, is almost exclusively concerned with extolling what he considers the usefulness of such failures: "For failure is really an essential part of the business of the United Nations."

The organization's importance to the world had thus shifted, in the view of its advocates, from the value of its mere continued existence, applauded in the nineteen-seventies, to a newly propounded and "essential" concept of failure. Under this new teaching, any United Nations potential for moral leadership is, moreover, quite discarded.

The public has found it less easy to exclude from consideration, as O'Brien does, the victims of this policy of failure. Beyond the "twenty million" fatalities relegated by O'Brien to unpondered oblivion, the era since the Second World War has encompassed the displacement of entire populations, the invasion and violent destruction of ancient societies and cultures, and the mutual expansion of anarchy and authoritarianism—nearly all of this occurring without intervention, or even discussion, by the United Nations. Since 1945, many more than twenty million persons have lived in the clutch of arbitrary rule, under threat of torture, detention, and death, uncomforted by any gesture from the vast organization whose solemn duty it is—under such covenants as the Universal Declaration of Human Rights—to speak in their defense. The most fearful aspect of this chaos is its growth and acceleration. Its foremost victim is civilization.

There is no evidence that the United Nations' shoddiness found "probably preferable" by Conor Cruise O'Brien—who holds over us, should we disagree with his cruel and tendentious argument, the threat of Armageddon—has been the sole alternative to global extinction, or that the interest of the great powers in avoiding confrontation could have been served only by such an unwieldy, inept, and often foolish instrument as the present United Nations. Nor need we assume that citizens will indefinitely extend and embellish the life of an organism, unresponsive to contemporary opportunities and dangers and indifferent to its own quality, whose degree of usefulness exists in huge disproportion to its resources and potential. What political utility the United Nations has shown over the past quarter century has allowed humanity to glimpse, merely, far greater possibilities inherent in the suppressed power of a concept that now cries out for invigoration, and for new and rational forms.

As the Waldheim era closed at the U.N., however, the world's public was urged by prominent commentators to swallow its misgivings—and, indeed, its instincts for decency and common sense. And, in February, 1982, shortly after Waldheim's departure from the United Nations, a New York *Times* editorial, which opened by deploring the futility of U.N. proceedings, concluded with the assertion "If every year's palaver produced one good idea and suffocated a dozen of the bad, boredom should be tolerable." No other great public institution has received such indulgence.

11

ON JANUARY 17, 1986, six weeks before the evidence of Waldheim's concealed activities under Hitler appeared in the world's press, an extensive appreciation, by Conor Cruise O'Brien, of Waldheim's character and Secretary-Generalship was published in the *Times Literary Supplement* under the title "The Very Model of a Secretary-General." O'Brien, whose long association with United Nations affairs includes Secretariat service, seized the occasion of reviewing Waldheim's memoirs, *In the Eye of the Storm*, to expound his enthusiasm for the former Secretary-General's performance in his U.N. post. O'Brien's essay has importance not only because it corresponds to the conception of the U.N.'s role dictated to us, with the same assurance, by United Nations spokesmen of the past quarter century but because it epitomizes that favorable view of Kurt Waldheim which—although it would soon be abandoned—had been propounded by U.N. leaders for many years; and which indubitably would yet hold sway had it not been for the irruption of momentous and irrefutable truth.

In his article O'Brien, having sought to neutralize skepticism with some introductory derision of Waldheim's charm-less persona, quickly warmed to his theme—his conviction that the reliable qualities he had long distinguished in Kurt Waldheim, and Waldheim's capacity for inspiring trust, were admirable attributes in a United Nations leader: "With Wald-heim, you knew where you were; with Waldheim there would be no surprises." And O'Brien deplored the Chinese veto that deprived us of a third Waldheim term. There is grim enter-tainment in this, even if—as O'Brien merrily remarks of Waldheim's own writings—"the entertainment is not always intentional." O'Brien, no less than Waldheim—although pre-sumably from different causes—is mesmerized by negation. Referring to Waldheim's postwar recruitment into the Aus-trian Foreign Affairs Ministry, headed by Karl Gruber, O'Brien tells us: "The grounds for Gruber's esteem, reported by Waldheim, are significant. 'If Waldheim tells me we can't do anything about a problem, I believe him.' So," O'Brien continues, "from the beginning of his career, Waldheim's strong suit was already apparent in his respect for *limits*."

It will be remembered that Waldheim himself, at the time of his election to the United Nations post in 1971, had drawn governmental attention to his particular grasp of lim-its. And that Joseph Kraft, in his prompt and prescient con-demnation of Waldheim's appointment, had noted this fact in a spirit that has, in contrast to O'Brien's, been fully vindi-cated. That limitation is not always an arbitrary factor, and that the boundaries conceived by Waldheim and O'Brien might, to a more detached or visionary observer, appear sus-ceptible of extension, is not considered by O'Brien in his 1986 article; nor does he give thought to the possibility that

Waldheim's phenomenal caution may be dictated by elements of which he, O'Brien, is ignorant. His tone is hectoring: we are to understand—as it were, once and for all—that in most issues coming before it there was "nothing much the U.N. could do" other than provide a sounding board and some relief services (services that would, in fact, in many instances not have been required had the U.N. been able to realize its potential); that any perceptible initiative from U.N. leaders might dangerously "rock the boat"; and that the principal task of a Secretary-General is to ingratiate himself with governments, in particular with those of the great powers.

O'Brien, like Urquhart, felt that Waldheim had been underestimated. Like Urquhart, he favorably contrasted Waldheim's "discretion"—"such habits of discretion that in the end you can no longer be revealing even when you decide to write your memoirs"—with what he saw as the provocative activism of Dag Hammarskjöld's Secretary-Generalship, pointing to the dénouement of Hammarskjöld's difficulties in the post-colonial chaos of the Congo, as if that nullified his previous achievements. It was presumably to such an attitude that Hammarskjöld had addressed himself in 1957, on his unanimous reëlection to a second term at the United Nations: "If a mountain wall is once climbed, later failures do not undo the fact that it has been shown that it *can* be climbed."

Almost from the moment of his death, in 1961, Hammarskjöld had been cited in United Nations circles as an aberration, not an exemplar. With the Waldheim years, however, allusion to Hammarskjöld acquired, at the U.N., a persistent note of disparagement as the effort to rationalize the organization's abnegations under Waldheim exacted some repudiation of Hammarskjöld's contrasting resourcefulness. In the New York *Times Magazine* of September 13, 1981, Brian Urquhart had decried what he felt was an excessive public appreciation of Hammarskjöld: "Everybody now thinks of Hammarskjöld as a huge success. The fact is that he became a total lame duck. The Russians and the French wouldn't speak to him and a lot of other people didn't want anything to do with him. By the end of his tenure he was out." And Urquhart went on, in the same article, to state his conviction that "in terms of usefulness, not glamor," Kurt Waldheim had "actually been the best Secretary-General."

12

WHILE ENCOMIUMS APPEARED in the press, pronounced by advocates who at times seemed crazed with self-justification, the mismanagement of the organization—confirmed in a flow of internal and ineffective reports—could not be concealed from its personnel. The entrenched concept of establishment allegiance and reverence for the Secretary-General, the promptings of self-interest, and the system of political favor governing senior appointments to the United Nations staff precluded the likelihood of resistance to policies of the Waldheim era in the upper levels of the Secretariat. In the remaining segment of the staff, intimidation and bureaucratic conformity had long reduced the spirit not of resentment but of opposition. The multiplying abuses of these years, however, and their dangerous consequences for U.N. personnel, revived a decent unrest in some members of those intermediate and junior grades where selection was not yet entirely dominated by geographical and political lottery.

In 1976, as Kurt Waldheim travelled the world in search of governmental support for his reëlection, a near-hiatus of leadership intensified the demoralization of headquarters personnel. Given the Secretary-General's dubious conduct of his office, the long dissatisfaction of the staff could at this juncture have been rallied—had it received even token support from U.N. leaders—as a factor against Waldheim's second election. Senior United Nations officials who in those years lobbied intensively with governments—and particularly with United States authorities—for increased funds for rival U.N. programs might have turned their efforts to making known, in government circles, the wide distaste felt for Waldheim's leadership by the U.N. service itself. That such possibilities of concerted expression on a vital matter were never even entertained is indicative of the Secretariat's weakness. In the autumn of that year, General Assembly delegates themselves showed disinclination to shoulder the blame mechanically attributed to them by Secretariat leaders—a United States representative, Mrs. Ersa H. Poston, laying responsibility for Secretariat chaos at Waldheim's door and citing his unbounded accessibility to national pressures.

In December, 1976, Kurt Waldheim was elected to his second U.N. term. The New York *Times* greeted the event warmly in an editorial and also reported that "the United States delegate, William W. Scranton, hailed Mr. Waldheim's reelection, saying he would have 'another excellent term' and adding: 'This will be important to the high standing of the United Nations, which he has always upheld.' Similar support came from members of the Soviet delegation."

During Waldheim's second term, staff representatives, led by Lowell Flanders, a young American in a junior professional post at the Secretariat, struggled to redress the adverse

107

state of the international civil service. Thwarted in their negotiations with the United Nations administration, they attempted to bring the Secretariat's condition to responsible attention—by such recourse to the press as U.N. restrictions allow, by individual meetings with the envoys of the "more serious" member states, and by formal appeals to appropriate bodies of the General Assembly. (A 1950 attempt, by staff representatives, to bring their complaints against the first Secretary-General, Trygve Lie, to Assembly attention had infuriated the organization's leaders, who, openly threatening reprisal, sought to frustrate it. Staff spokesmen were enabled to express their disquiet to the Assembly during the latter Waldheim years by a special provision enacted by the Assembly itself in consequence of staff agitation.) All these efforts failed in their object—of generating wide concern and consequent reforms: the public remained unaware of the scale and intensity of staff discontent with the United Nations leadership. The spectacle, however, of a staff body vainly seeking the proper use of its resources in the organization's service and soliciting, in effect, the intercession of the organization's governing council to prevent continued mismanagement by its appointed leaders was not new at the United Nations.

The documented account of the staff's relations with the U.N. administration provides, as yet, the only candid record of the organization's inner life during its years under Waldheim. The plight of the Secretariat staff was also set forth in those years in academic and internal studies—notably, in 1977, by Theodor Meron, of the New York University School of Law, in his book *The United Nations Secretariat*—but such appeals and warnings rarely came to public notice; and were, among the U.N. leadership, entirely disregarded.

In the late nineteen-seventies, the U.N. staff union in New York engaged the American labor negotiator Theodore Kheel to represent it in its dealings with the U.N. administration. Kheel—worldly, skeptical, confident, and an unlikely audience for the condescension of U.N. leaders—had also represented staff interests at the European office of the U.N. in Geneva, and he accepted the assignment for a nominal fee. His experience with the United Nations hierarchy—which he likened to "the court of King Henry VIII"—and in particular with its propensity for abrogating formal agreements on basic matters of staff rights—moved him, in an interview with Morton Mintz, in the Washington *Post* on February 18, 1979, to compare Waldheim unfavorably with Jimmy Hoffa, the late chief of the Teamsters union: "Every employer said that Hoffa may be a bum, a thief, but that if he gives you his word, he honors it."

"The thing that utterly amazed me," Kheel said in 1989, "was the position taken by the Secretary-General of the United Nations to disregard the elementary established rights of employees: that the agency created to maintain standards of human decency and to bring about peace by negotiated settlement would violate its own agreements and see no necessity for compliance with its own word."

Like others before him, Kheel noted the effect, on the organization's potential, of a demoralized Secretariat, remarking, in 1980, of Waldheim's foredoomed overtures to Iran in the hostage crisis: "Waldheim would be a better international mediator if he'd eschew the role of ayatollah toward his own staff."

The correspondence between Theodore Kheel, on the one hand, and Kurt Waldheim and his legal officers, on the other, is again a significant record of the organization's mood in those years, and of its attitude to its legal and ethical obligations. Kheel observed of his attempts to negotiate with the Secretary-General, "He answered by not responding to the points I made and deliberately refusing my persistent efforts to get him to respond." This was not to be the last example of Waldheim's recourse to that technique.

In August, 1979, Alicja Wesolowska, a young Polish member of the United Nations staff, was detained by Polish authorities as she visited friends in Warsaw en route to a U.N. assignment in Mongolia. Held incommunicado until the following March, she was then convicted, in a closed military court, of having "contacts with foreign intelligence." The charge, for which no evidence was produced, was apparently without substance; and is thought to represent retaliation, by the Polish government of that era, against Wesolowska's show of independence from Soviet-bloc pressures during her United Nations employment. It should not, in any case, have affected her right to due process. She received a sentence of seven years.

Alicja Wesolowska's detention and trial occurred in flagrant violation of her elementary rights, and of United Nations covenants, to which Poland is a signatory, regarding the rights and immunities of international civil servants. In this episode, the Secretary-General showed himself without influence and extremely reluctant to assert principles that touched the safety and standing of every U.N. employee, including himself. Only as a result of insistent staff protests, and of public pressure as the story was aired in the Western press, was Waldheim induced to make a minimal appeal to the Polish authorities. While one must wonder whether his unwillingness to articulate principle in this basic case was linked to fear, it must be said that United Nations reports on conditions of human rights in Poland, submitted after Waldheim's departure, consistently minimized the Polish government's violations in the years of Solidarity's hardest struggle; and that in the Wesolowska episode Waldheim's senior circle presented, as ever, a united front with the Secretary-General.

Investigations, by staff representatives, into the case of Wesolowska brought to light about twenty other instances of U.N. employees who, undefended and unreported by the administration, had been arbitrarily seized and imprisoned while on assignment. These developments precipitated, on December 6, 1979, a crowded rally of Secretariat staff for the purpose of making—for the first time in many years—a concerted appeal to the U.N. leadership for a return to the founding principles of the international civil service. One of the most significant meetings held at the United Nations during the Waldheim decade, this solemn gathering was unnoticed in the press—being reported by the New York *Times* two months later, on February 14, 1980, only in consequence of a vehement Soviet protest over the event. Soon after this rally, a staff representative was summoned by one of Waldheim's chief deputies, who cautioned him to leave the matter to the Secretary-General. Staff leaders, however, continued to press for the restoration of Wesolowska's rights.

Alicja Wesolowska served nearly five years of her sentence. Following her release, she eventually received from the United Nations an assignment to a hardship mission in central Africa. Declining this assignment, and expressing her wish to resume her duties in New York, she instead received instructions to join another field mission, in Cyprus. As she now required medical treatment, this proved impossible. Although it was made clear to her that her presence at headquarters would be intolerable to the United Nations administration because of pressure from the Polish government—Poland then being under authoritarian rule—she made her way to New York in 1986; and there underwent medical treatment. Her efforts to rejoin the United Nations headquarters staff, to which she still officially belonged, were countered with attempts by the U.N. administration to dispatch her to field assignments, and with the proposal to demote her from professional duties to a typing post. In 1989, her resistance at an end, she accepted—in the U.N. phrase—an "agreed termination." United Nations' subservience to totalitarian rulers in Poland thus persisted to the very eve of that country's emancipation from Soviet control, heedless of the tide of world events.

Of the numerous other U.N. employees missing on field assignments, several are believed to have died in prison. In the past decade, such cases have apparently tripled, without effective intervention by the United Nations administration.

13

A LIE, having no reality, is difficult to repeat with consistency. And Kurt Waldheim, in the accounts of his past offered during his U.N. tenure, had plainly signalled, if not the truth of his years under Hitler, at least the areas of concealment. Even his assertion, from the time of his United Nations appointment, that he had been invalided out of the German Army at the end of 1941 with a wound received on the Russian front, and had then pursued his studies at Vienna until 1945, was subject to variation in dates and theatres of war service. In his early years at the U.N., Waldheim was circumspect in allusions to the events of his youth—mere reference to which by others was greeted as an offense by his U.N. deputies. (Objecting to an exposition, by the present writer, in the New York *Times Book Review* of August 25, 1974, of United Nations acts of censorship against Aleksandr Solzhenitsyn, the Secretary-General's official spokesman deplored public mention even of war service that Waldheim himself had not denied: "In addition, Shirley Hazzard refers to Mr. Waldheim as 'an officer in Hitler's army on the Russian front,' which is a very injurious accusation, and can only lead

113

the readers of this article to have adverse feelings toward the Secretary-General." The reference in question was not, of course, an "accusation" but a statement of uncontested fact.)

As Waldheim's story went unchallenged, however, throughout his first years at the United Nations, he was emboldened; and began to allude freely to the admitted portion of his early experience, and even to elaborate his previous account with inventions and additions that, while casting him in a favorable or pathetic light, sailed ever closer to the wind. In the years following his election to a second term at the U.N., Waldheim, in his public remarks, provided numerous clues to his past life; and, to a curious extent, told his hidden story in the press.

As reported in an interview in 1975, by Barbara Kerr, for *People* magazine, Waldheim's "law studies were interrupted by the fascist takeover of Austria in 1938 when his father, a civil servant and anti-Nazi leader, was jailed for two years." (It will be recalled that, following the Anschluss, Waldheim's father, who had been a political adherent of the conservative nationalist Kurt von Schuschnigg, was dismissed from his post as a school superintendent. He was detained by the Nazis, on more than one occasion, for a period of hours or days.) The article continued: "In 1942 [on the Russian front] a grenade exploded near Kurt's right leg, and he was sent home. 'It saved my life.' He could not walk normally for a year, but was able to resume his law courses at the university where he met his future wife. . . . 'Our young years were not easy. Do you know that my wife never went to a ball as a young woman. Never! For me it was the same.' "

In his autobiography, *In the Eye of the Storm*, published in the United States early in 1986, Waldheim asserts that, following his wound, "it took several months in a sanatorium in the mountains before my leg started to heal properly. I walked with a bad limp, and to my undisguised relief was discharged from further service at the front. I made a formal request to be permitted to resume my law studies and take my Master's degree and, rather to my surprise, this was granted. I still had my pay as a lieutenant and this helped to see me through. . . . It was impossible to leave Austria." According to recent research, Waldheim was wounded on the Russian front on December 14, 1941. After two months' convalescence, he reported to his unit at the beginning of March, 1942; and was ordered to Belgrade, where he took up his new duties on March 14th.

During his U.N. years, in two particular interviews—published respectively in the Washington *Post* of January 18, 1980, and the New York *Times Magazine* of September 13, 1981—Waldheim seemed to be courting exposure. The *Post* quoted him as saying:

> Very soon I was wounded on the east front and that probably saved my life. I couldn't walk for a long time and I was released from active service in 1941.

The *Times* stated:

> Mr. Waldheim says that his father, a conservative Roman Catholic school official, spoke out publicly against the Nazis, and he himself joined the anti-Nazi Austrian Youth Movement. . . . At the beginning of World War II, young Kurt was drafted into the German Army. "Fortunately," Mr. Waldheim says, "I didn't last long. My unit moved to the Russian front in the winter of 1942. I was

115

badly wounded in the ankle, I couldn't walk, and they gave me a medical discharge."

In these extensive interviews, Waldheim restated the false version of his war service in uncompromising if divergent terms. The tardy innovation of his membership in "the anti-Nazi Austrian Youth Movement" was still more audacious. It is clear that Waldheim, had he belonged to any organization dedicated to resisting Nazi rule, would have flourished that fact throughout his postwar career, rather than disclosing it in an aside at the end of his decade at the United Nations. (In his autobiography Waldheim makes passing reference to his youthful membership, before the Anschluss, in an Austrian youth group supporting Kurt von Schuschnigg; and this is echoed, but not developed, in the "white book" prepared, in 1987, in Waldheim's defense by officials of the Austrian Foreign Affairs Ministry. It is possible that support prior to the Anschluss for a conservative nationalist and his party has been given the complexion of a post-Anschluss resistance to the evil doctrines of Nazism.) It is also apparent that a young man with such a record, who had been—as he asserted—"harassed continuously by the Gestapo," would not have been appointed a staff officer in the German Army, and in an Intelligence position, without first tendering firm evidence of his acceptance of Nazi precepts. Waldheim's claim to organized anti-Nazi activity, which might have been challenged at once by some informed reader of the interview, was refuted by Hillel Seidman, a survivor and scholar of the Nazi persecutions and one of the first writers to probe Waldheim's deceptions. In 1982, in his book *United Nations: Perfidy and*

Perversion, Dr. Seidman reported that "the anti-Nazi Austrian Youth Movement" had never existed. No attention was
paid at the U.N. to this disclosure, or to other clear indications of Waldheim's untruthfulness.

Waldheim told the Washington *Post* that "my father
wanted me to be a doctor and I refused. I said, 'Daddy, I
cannot see blood.' " The interview resumed: "After Waldheim got out of the German army he continued his studies
and met his wife at that time. 'After that, things went perfectly well.' " Waldheim met his future wife, Elisabeth
Ritschel, in the winter of 1942–43, when he returned on
leave to Vienna from his duties with the German Intelligence
staff at Arsakli, near the port city of Salonika. (Salonika's
Jewish population of fifty thousand would be, by mid-1943,
almost entirely deported by the Germans—a crime with
which, according to the researches of the historian Robert
Herzstein, Waldheim was apparently unconnected.) Elisabeth Ritschel was the daughter of a staunch Nazi; and, at the
time of her meeting with Waldhcim, she had—as she acknowledged to the press in June, 1986—herself been a member of the Nazi Party for more than a year. Before his posting
to the environs of Salonika, Waldheim had been assigned to
a German assault on Yugoslav partisans on the Kozara pla-
teau, in West Bosnia. Waldheim's precise association with
the Kozara operation, which culminated in the massacre or
deportation of tens of thousands of civilians, is not known.
His own statements regarding it are contradictory. In April,
1943, following his leave in Vienna, Waldheim returned to
active duty in the Balkans, where renewed German on-
slaughts against resistance fighters, and the events of the im-

minent Italian collapse, would combine to create one of the
bloodiest phases of the war. It is in this period of his life, by
Waldheim's account, that "things went perfectly well."

It is hard not to see, in the risks gratuitously taken by
Waldheim in making assertions that flew in the face of
history, a compulsion to test his fate. Bizarre also are Waldheim's allusions (conspicuous in the Washington *Post* interview, in which his wife emphatically participated) to hidden
aspects of his life—allusions to be appreciated only by the
one other person cognizant of the truth:

> People of course now see me as Secretary-General in this
> interesting function, important, etcetera, but who knows
> what I went through until I reached that point?

The interviewer, ingenuously noting that "it is hard to find
much material on Waldheim," recalls, "Above all, Waldheim is a man who once said, 'Long experience has taught me
that an abrupt gesture, an ill-chosen word or an unthinking
remark can prove disastrous.' "

A curious feature of the Waldheim imposture has been the
complicity of husband and wife in their long agreement to lie
without compunction, to counter truth with a show of histrionic outrage, and to live continually in the shadow of a traumatic unmasking. In this aspect of their story we draw near to
its inner, Dickensian reality—as when, in *Our Mutual
Friend*, the ruthless Lammles, of "shining reputation," exchange one candid glance in a mirror: "Next moment they
quietly eyed each other, as if they, the principals, had had no
part in that expressive transaction."

14

On November 26, 1980, a United States representative, Stephen J. Solarz—prompted by his constituents, and by Hillel Seidman—wrote to Kurt Waldheim, at the United Nations, and to the director of the Central Intelligence Agency, in Washington, requesting information on Waldheim's activities under Hitler. This inquiry was made in the wake of an article in *The New Republic* of January 19th of that year, in which the present writer stated that Waldheim had been a member of Nazi groups and had served in the German Army "in various campaigns" of the Second World War; and of a further assertion, by Martin Peretz, editor-in-chief and publisher of *The New Republic*, in the same magazine on September 27, 1980, affirming that Waldheim had belonged to the Nazi movement.

On December 19th, Waldheim replied. Dismissing the statements in *The New Republic* as "slanders," and noting that the president of the United Nations Association of the United States had characterized my own assertion as a "McCarthyesque lie," he went on to offer the following equivocation:

You will, I am sure, agree with me that it would be odd, to say the least, if the government of the United States and all other Member Governments voted twice to elect me as Secretary-General of the United Nations if they had been in any doubt as to my character and background.

It is indeed odd, to say the least. It is one of the oddest circumstances of a singular era.

Waldheim's deflection of responsibility to the national agencies charged with investigating him, and the citation of their endorsement—or complicity—as proof of his rectitude, was a bold card he would play again. In March, 1986, as details of Waldheim's concealed past under Hitler appeared in the Western press, the *International Herald Tribune* reported:

> Mr. Waldheim said he had been checked by the secret services of all major powers before he became U.N. secretary-general in 1972, and he asked how they would have passed him for the post if he had been found to have "a single brown spot."

In his December, 1980, letter to Solarz, Waldheim proceeded to state that he had never been associated in any way with the Nazi Youth Movement; and to repeat the fiction that his war wound, sustained on the Russian front, had incapacitated him for military service after 1941. We may imagine with what reluctance Waldheim made this first formal written commitment to his long imposture.

Despite that denial, and his characterization of *The New Republic*'s references to his concealed past as slanderous, Waldheim took no legal step against the magazine or the authors of these articles; nor did he request a retraction of the statements at issue. As the charges were repeated, however, in an uncompromising article, in *The New Republic* of March 7, 1981, again by Martin Peretz, Waldheim did seek through a private emissary to intimidate the magazine with the threat of a possible libel suit. Peretz has recounted his response: "That if Waldheim sued us, he would find himself in discovery proceedings. That was the last we heard about a libel suit. Now we know why."

In his memoirs Waldheim reports that, at "a personal, private meeting" with Solarz, arranged as a result of Solarz's concern, "I explained my background in detail to the Congressman." That explanation presumably recounted some version of Waldheim's fictitious history. (In April, 1986, after Waldheim's story had been revealed in the press, Solarz would again write to Waldheim, to demand an explanation of his compounded deception; and would receive a reply of unregenerate falsehood.)

On December 31, 1980, the Legislative Counsel of the Central Intelligence Agency had replied to Representative Solarz, acknowledging his request and stating: "We believe that Waldheim was not a member of the Nazi Youth Movement, nor was he involved in anti-Jewish activities. We have no intelligence reporting in detail on Waldheim's military service." The letter went on to echo—as "gleaned" from "German open source materials"—Waldheim's own version of his military career.

The vagueness of the C.I.A., although matched by the incuriosity of the United Nations, was in contrast to intuitive as well as informed doubts raised outside official circles at that time by Waldheim's personality and conduct, and by the evident lacunae in his story. Graham Greene, writing to me on January 17, 1981, with regard to "that awful man at the head of the United Nations," observed, "I notice that Kurt Waldheim omits from *Who's Who* whatever career he had between 1939 and 1945. Can you give me details? Why does he omit all this from *Who's Who*?" Had Waldheim, as he claimed, attended a university from 1941 until the close of the war, that fact would have been eagerly recorded in his written rather than merely in his oral statements.

In the last years of Waldheim's Secretary-Generalship, the absence of U.N. initiatives in the world's crises was increasingly viewed by thoughtful citizens as dangerous and incomprehensible. Breaking out of the web of U.N. excuse, the more reflective elements of the world's press also began to seek the meaning of the organization's passivity, and to trace Waldheim's role in it. In October, 1979, deploring the tragic condition of Cambodia, the British newspaper the *Guardian* observed:

> As so often when anything important is taking place in the world, the U.N. itself is silent. It is aided, abetted and guided in that silence by the inactivity of the Secretary-General himself. . . . Why does not Kurt Waldheim make a strenuous effort to overcome the deadly punctilio in which his office has taken refuge?

15

In 1981, Kurt Waldheim again travelled the world seeking governmental support for a renewed term at the United Nations. In the summer of that year, the New York *Times* reported that he "came back, according to aides, with only one outright promise of support, from Lord Carrington, the British Foreign Secretary. . . . In the other capitals, save Peking, heads of governments gave Mr. Waldheim the diplomatic equivalents of nods and winks to let him know they would not oppose his bid. In Moscow, *Pravda* coupled his name approvingly with that of Leonid I. Brezhnev and cited their joint efforts in seeking peace." Two years earlier, Soviet troops had entered Afghanistan, where they would remain for a decade.

The *Times*—which had reported concern over the Secretary-General's "active campaigning"—found that "at the higher levels of the United Nations Secretariat he has more defenders than critics."

In late 1981, as the Security Council took up the election of a new Secretary-General, Waldheim had the support of four of its five permanent members: Britain, France, the Soviet Union, and the United States. The fifth member, the government of China—explaining that "China has no personal prejudice against Waldheim" but could not accept manipulation "by one or two superpowers"—used its power of veto against Waldheim's bid for a third term. "Through that Chinese *coup de grâce*," Conor Cruise O'Brien would subsequently write, "the United Nations lost a diplomatist, and an international civil servant, of great experience." The loss was not widely felt outside the organization, or in the staff body.

The new, and fifth, Secretary-General, Javier Pérez de Cuéllar, came—like his three immediate predecessors—from a long official connection with the United Nations and its Secretariat. And, as in the case of his precursor, Kurt Waldheim, Pérez de Cuéllar's election was greeted as confirmation of an established pattern—the New York *Times* reporting, of the new Secretary-General, that "his favorite word is 'caution.' "

It had been conjectured that Waldheim, in retirement, would assume some role with the international community at Vienna, where, during his Secretary-Generalship, United Nations offices had swelled to a veritable city along the Danube. This did not occur. In 1983, Waldheim helped to organize a group called the International Council of Former Heads of Government, the declared purpose of which was to offer experienced counsel to incumbent world leaders. Its thirty members did not include former leaders of the United States or the Soviet Union. To Waldheim, long swaddled in the self-importance of the U.N. cocoon and eager for the prominence of public office, such a group—with its suggestion of superannuation or rejection—must have seemed merely a provisional setting. In 1986, he was supported by the conservative People's Party as a prospective candidate for the largely ceremonial office of President of Austria. As a candidate of the same party, he had lost the Presidential election in 1971; and from that defeat had gone on to become Secretary-General of the United Nations.

With Waldheim's renewed nomination for the Austrian Presidency, his early record attracted, from his political opponents in particular, a degree of attention that it had not received in his years at the United Nations. On March 3, 1986, nine weeks before the Presidential election, the Austrian magazine *Profil* published the first detailed revelations—by Hubertus Czernin, who would subsequently write at length on the matter—of Waldheim's concealed past. The following day, the New York *Times* reported in detail Waldheim's prewar membership in two Nazi-affiliated groups and his involvement in Hitler's campaign in the Balkans; and the story was aired around the world. Of these disclosures, Waldheim declared, "The timing of it is perfect. For forty years these things have rested." While the timing was in fact ordered by Waldheim himself, who had had forty years in which to tell the truth, it is undeniable that matters resolutely ignored throughout Waldheim's decade at the United Nations were sifted and found imperative when he sought his new office in the broader light of "the real world."

Of his membership in Nazi groups, Waldheim, who had formerly and indignantly denied such a connection, now responded, "And even if it were true, well, so what?" In the ensuing days, he explained to an interviewer that he had not previously recounted these matters because they were "too boring." Of German atrocities against partisans and civilians during the Balkans campaign, he later observed, "I also knew that many German soldiers were trapped and executed in a similar way."

"There is a manner of doing evil," Anthony Trollope observed, "so easy and indifferent as absolutely to quell the general feeling respecting it. A man shall tell you that he has committed a murder in a tone so careless as to make you feel that a murder is nothing." Such a spell is cast with some frequency over the modern electorate. After failing to obtain the required majority at the polls in May, Kurt Waldheim was elected President of Austria in a runoff on June 8, 1986, receiving almost fifty-four per cent of the vote. He was then sixty-seven years old.

16

SINCE TRUTH WAS SET in motion regarding Kurt Waldheim's past, his former associates at the U.N. have discussed his character in new and adverse terms. Brian Urquhart, who in the wake of Waldheim's exposure has described his former chief's "insatiable ambition for public-office," "monstrous ego," and "hide of a rhinoceros," speaks in his recent memoirs of "fantasies" apparently entertained among Waldheim's senior colleagues at the United Nations:

> We saw him as two people: Waldheim Mark I, a scheming, ambitious, duplicitous egomaniac ready to do anything for advantage or public acclaim; and Waldheim Mark II, the statesmanlike leader who kept his head while all about him were losing theirs and was prepared to follow our advice in great international crises. These and other fantasies seem rather less funny now.

The world's public, being provided by United Nations spokesmen with only the second of these supposed fantasies, had no means of challenging the reality. Urquhart has related elsewhere that, having been assured by Waldheim himself, in his United Nations years, that published references to the Secretary-General's hidden past were unfounded, "I accepted his answers as being true, not believing that anyone who had attained a position of such responsibility would lie about a matter of such importance." Reverence for position, injurious to every aspect of United Nations activity, in this case seems to have imposed an unusual degree of credulity; and one must wonder, by extension, if this is the spirit in which United Nations negotiations are carried on with heads of government. It would be hard to discover elsewhere, in the public of the post-Watergate age, such unquestioning trust in the word of elected leaders. In any case, Waldheim had already given ample evidence of his untruthfulness, not only in divergent and sometimes fanciful accounts of his own past, but in public statements concerned with U.N. policies, above all in the field of human rights.

* In March, 1988—as, at the fiftieth anniversary of the Anschluss, thousands of Austrians themselves called for Waldheim's resignation—two notable condemnations of Waldheim appeared in letters published in the British newspaper the *Independent*. Both letters touch profoundly on the public's inability to obtain timely information, and to form accurate impressions, regarding the United Nations.

Robert Rhodes James, a Member of Parliament and a former official of the United Nations, stated with reference to Waldheim's comments in a press interview:

> Waldheim described me as "sort of a speechwriter." In fact, in addition to my other duties as principal officer in his executive office for 10 years, I was his only speechwriter. It was not a pleasant assignment, but my task—on

behalf of the U.N.—was to stop the Secretary-General consistently making a fool of himself, or, much more important, the world organization.

We were not always successful. . . . Waldheim was certainly "a sort of Secretary-General" of the most loathsome kind.

He is now "a sort of President of Austria" and they are welcome to him. Had it not been for the Chinese refusal to tolerate him anymore, he would still be Secretary-General of the U.N.—his election supported by the British Government, in spite of my vehement objections—so this appalling situation would be even worse than it is.

Brian Urquhart, in a moment of moderation, has described Waldheim as "a duplicitous egomaniac." As Brian's platoon was the first to arrive at Belsen, his self restraint is remarkable.

Following the documented revelations of Waldheim's past, Robert Rhodes James became chairman of a British Parliamentary committee to investigate the former Secretary-General's wartime history. Rhodes James's above letter, of March, 1988, was endorsed in the *Independent* by George Ivan Smith, a former prominent official of the United Nations:

Robert Rhodes James describes Waldheim as "a sort of Secretary-General of a most loathsome kind." I agree, as the senior Australian having served at the highest non-political level on the U.N. Secretariat. . . .

It is proper now that Waldheim's inglorious record at the U.N. should be examined. He and his supporters are using his imagined international distinction as a shield to protect his domestic political base . . . but Waldheim must not be allowed to pretend that he served the United Nations with distinction. He brought it to unprecedented

crisis, financially and politically, shattered the morale
of a dedicated international secretariat, variously offended
governments and correspondents with gusts of misjudgment and uncontrolled temperament that often ended
in public screams of rage. . . .

He is the only incumbent to have lobbied for the
post. He is the only one suspected of having tied a
number of senior appointments to the votes given in
his support by their countries of origin.

Kurt Waldheim's "imagined international distinction" was
presumably invented, in the first instance, by his spokesmen
at the United Nations—not least, one must assume, by "his
only speechwriter." Endorsement of Waldheim's conduct of
his office was adhered to, over years, by his senior colleagues, in the face of public doubts and staff protests to
which no United Nations leader lent even transient solidarity;
and in disregard of the Secretariat's "unprecedented crisis"
and of Waldheim's violations of United Nations precepts.
Just as Waldheim, even yet, might resign his present office
and withdraw into decent obscurity, so truth can be served by
an admission of error on the part of those who persistently
supported him, and who have not—in these late excoria-
tions—acknowledged or explained their roles. Why "it is
proper now that Waldheim's inglorious record at the U.N.
should be examined" yet was not found appropriate by these
same deputies while that record was being—against the public interest but "on behalf of the United Nations"—disas-
trously created is a bureaucratic riddle easily solved, perhaps, in the public mind.

The strain of knowingness that tinges the inner circle of a

large organization contributed heavily, at the United Nations, to Waldheim's unimpeded career. Those in authority closed ranks as a privileged and authoritative body whose oracular pronouncements connoted absolute knowledge. A quarter century ago, Conor Cruise O'Brien could discuss with some detachment his own need—during Hammarskjöld's venture in the Congo—for the approval of this "inner circle of the Secretariat":

> What I was actually most conscious of was the more primitive feeling of pleasure at now being, as I thought, "on the inside" of this major international operation, combined with a sense of deflation, on realizing how very much "on the outside" one had been, as an ordinary delegate in the corridors of the Assembly and at the Advisory Committee.

Of the disorder that, in the Congo itself, subsequently overwhelmed him in its contradictions, O'Brien then candidly recounted:

> I was bewildered and depressed by the way in which . . . I had lost the rapport with headquarters which I had believed myself to possess up to then. I was rather childishly anxious to reinstate myself in their good graces.

In these conditions, where individual self-esteem is dependent on the approval of a privileged circle at the institution, rebuttal of independent opinions expressed by outsiders becomes mechanical, for such views appear to threaten the exclusivity of inside knowledge. At the United Nations, in the Waldheim period, the organization's leaders appeared not only to suspend belief in the possibility of illumination from outside U.N. walls but to consider any independent judgment concerning the institution as intrinsically misconceived and presumptuous. Thus, in the view of the initiates, the public, uninstructed, was "always underrating" Kurt Waldheim. Yet the world in general appraised Waldheim's character correctly, because vanity was not involved in its assessment.

Special knowledge, at the United Nations, foundered on the rock of the Waldheim case. Like all mankind in trouble, Waldheim's late apologists have sought comfort, on this issue at least, in their shared human fallibility, stressing that "like everyone else," or "like most people," they took Waldheim's statements at face value. The truth is, rather, that doubts about Waldheim's character were entertained and aired in many spheres outside the United Nations' inner circle. And members of the public bear no responsibility for promoting Waldheim before the world, or for issuing imperious denials of his failings.

17

In *The Quality of Mercy*, his study of international relief operations in Cambodia, William Shawcross relates that, in the course of his researches into the administration of such aid, he inquired for the "Historical Office" of the United Nations. In response to this request, Brian Urquhart, laughing, "said that in that whole vast building with its hundreds of offices, there was no room for such a place." Shawcross goes on to quote Urquhart: " 'There is no historian at the United Nations, because no two members here could possibly agree on what has happened, let alone on what should be recorded.' " Absence of, and antipathy to, objectively recorded history shapes the difficulties, and oppresses the future, of the United Nations. The Secretariat suffers drastically from a denial of experience that—established early with the exclusion, from U.N. accounts, of Trygve Lie's formative pact with the United States government—is now strangely exemplified in Waldheim's own story. As with that original betrayal of the international Secretariat by its first leader, so, with the Waldheim drama, the United Nations inexorably turns away from self-knowledge. How the organization acquired such a

133

Secretary-General, what agencies conspired in his acceptance, what favors were extended in return, what manner of men indulged and praised him—these are great questions for all the world; but most of all for the United Nations.

In regard to this huge institution created nearly half a century ago for the prevention and mediation of disputes, public expectations are now small. It is a measure of those reduced hopes that a United Nations terminal role in conflicts—which, with their millions of casualties and their store of misery and rancor, have endured twice as long as the First World War—should in recent years have been greeted as "success." With any such "conventional" hostilities, we may assume that ultimate exhaustion of the belligerents, together with the extraneous pressures and mutations of great power, will bring at last some form of quietus—as, in James Merrill's words, "Peace limps forward on a cane." In past ages, history could contemplate, if not with equanimity, those wars, so named, of thirty or one hundred years, in which hopes for mediation were crowned at last with a comparable "success." Such grim leisure is not at the disposal of the modern world.

The need for an eventual reconsideration and radical reconstitution of the United Nations concept was foreseen in the U.N.'s early years, and embraced by Dag Hammarskjöld, as an inevitable response to transformations in world conditions and to the realized experience of the organization itself. Such a reformation might with great advantage have been inaugurated twenty years ago, before the world entered fully into its present stage of crisis. In the years of lost opportunity, the need for a new, intelligible rendering of the concept of international negotiation has only become more clearly dependent on energies excluded from the present United Nations and its satellite interests. The very broaching of such an idea in realistic terms, let alone the proper pondering of its practical application, implies a maturity, and a receptivity to history, quite absent from a body whose intractable insistence on its own indispensability has so long precluded consideration of new forms of international negotiation matched to the modern age. To recognize the stagnation of the United Nations, we need only reflect on the complete exclusion of the organization from every aspect of the great events that swept Eastern Europe in the autumn of 1989—as the U.N. General Assembly met in New York, remote and irrelevant.

Dissolution of the existing United Nations, and reëmbodiment of its original precepts in a new and radically different organism, has been sporadically aired in recent years, outside the organization, as a remote possibility. Unknown, however, to the public, this idea has been more definitely advanced within United Nations walls, in recognition of the unfitness of the present organization and of its incapacity for serious reform. In 1985, at the conclusion of its seventeen-year survey of United Nations affairs, the U.N.'s Joint Inspection Unit offered, in a document entitled *Some Reflections on Reform of the United Nations*, its belief that "the time has come to begin to reflect in a serious and ambitious way on the definition of a third-generation World Organization." The document offers proposals that focus, "following the two unfinished experiments of the League of Nations and the United Nations," on "a third generation World Organization genuinely in keeping with the needs of the modern world." For all its omissions and disclaimers, its invincibly timid attitude to public engage-

135

ment, and its delusion that regeneration could—or would—be usefully considered by those associated with the present body, this study has importance as an act of recognition; and as an attempt to transcend the intellectual torpor of nearly half a century. So far as I can discover, its existence is generally unknown, even in U.N. circles; its recommendations have received no serious consideration from the organiztion's leaders.

Any new organization that is to contribute to the conduct of world affairs a meaning far beyond governmental maneuvering will be brought forth by public pressure stimulated by a new degree of anxiety and alarm—and even by the rightful and insistent hopes of a fresh generation. It will depend, as the United Nations has not done, on quality: on accountability to human reason and accessibility to public involvement; and on the individual distinction of its officers. Its architects should bear in mind that in 1945 the founders of the United Nations sought to guarantee the calibre and courage of the staff of a new "world organization." And that, in 1971, through the long effects of conspiracy and negligence, the U.N.'s highest office passed to "a lank, shallow, unsufficient man" (the words are Milton's): a leader who, as Conor Cruise O'Brien reports, embodied "exactly the combination of qualities which the super-powers agree in regarding as desirable in a Secretary-General of the United Nations." Such is the magnetic attraction, in our time, of prominence and mere position, with their reflected advantages of self-esteem, that this deceitful figure could be presented as a paragon, his very deficiencies exalted into talents, and his fawnings on tyrants rationalized as consummate diplomacy, throughout ten of this world's most cruel and dangerous years.

NOTES

CHAPTER 1

PAGE 1 *"Nations from time to time"*
Jakob Burckhardt, *Reflections on History* (London: George Allen & Unwin, 1943), p. 137.

1 *Gustave Flaubert wrote*
Letter from Gustave Flaubert to George Sand, Aug. 3, 1870, in *The Letters of Gustave Flaubert*, vol. 2, *1857–1880*, ed. Francis Steegmuller (Cambridge, Mass.: Harvard University Press, 1982), p. 156.

6 *"from beholding"*
John Milton, "The Reason of Church-Government urg'd against Prelaty," in *John Milton: Selected Prose*, ed. C. A. Patrides (Baltimore: Penguin Books, 1974), p. 59.

6 *the Preparatory Commission*
Report of the Preparatory Commission of the United Nations, 1945, p. 92, par. 57. (This paragraph was not included in the provisional staff rules issued in 1946. See U.N. document A/435.)

6 *the comprehensive regulations*
Comprehensive staff rules: U.N. documents SGB/81, Rule 56 (1948); ST/AFS/SGB/81/Rev. 1–3 (1951); ST/AFS/SGB/94 (1954).

6 *in the Brief on Behalf of Nineteen Applicants*
Frank J. Donner, Arthur Kinoy, Leonard B. Boudin,
Morris J. Kaplan, In the United Nations Administrative
Tribunal: Brief on Behalf of Nineteen Applicants (1953),
p. 105.

See also Shirley Hazzard, *Defeat of an Ideal: A Study
of the Self-Destruction of the United Nations* (Boston:
Atlantic–Little, Brown, 1973), chs. 1–3; Shirley Hazzard,
"The Betrayal of the Charter," *Times Literary Supplement*,
Sept. 17, 1982.

7 *a written secret agreement*
Activities of United States Citizens Employed by the
United Nations: Hearings before the Subcommittee to
Investigate the Administration of the Internal Security Act
and Other Internal Security Laws of the Committee on the
Judiciary, United States Senate, 82nd Congress, 2nd Session, Oct. 13, 14, 15, 23, 24; Nov. 11, 12; Dec. 1, 2, 10,
11, 17, 1952, pp. 267–305, 328–90; Appendices B, C,
D, E, with particular reference to Appendix D, sec. 2, pp.
415–16 ("Arrangements with U.N. for the Provision of
Information on U.S. Nationals" and "Outline of Recom-
mended Procedure"; hereinafter cited as McCarran Hearings.)

7 *in a front-page account*
New York *Times*, Mar. 12, 1947.

8 *as Lie reported in January, 1950*
U.N. press release SG/43, Jan. 17, 1950; U.N. document
SCC/68, Jan. 19, 1950.

8 *in March, 1950*
Brief on Behalf of Nineteen Applicants, pp. 202–3.

9 *"the prevention and removal of threats to the peace"*
Charter of the United Nations, ch. 1, art. 1, 1.

9 *Secretary-General whose own initiatives*
Charter of the United Nations, ch. 15, art. 99.

9 *As Evan Luard*
Evan Luard, *A History of the United Nations*, vol. 1, *The Years of Western Domination, 1945–1955* (London: Macmillan, 1982), p. 117.

9 *John Maynard Keynes had acknowledged*
John Maynard Keynes, *The Economic Consequences of the Peace* (London: Macmillan, 1971), pp. 164–165.

11 *Articles 100 and 101 of the Charter*
Charter of the United Nations, ch. 15, arts. 100, 101.

11 *As Joseph P. Lash would observe*
New York *Post*, Dec. 12, 1952, p. 3.

11 *the experience of the League of Nations*
U.N. document 1155, 1/2/74(2), June 22, 1945, UNCIO, p. 394; and Brief on Behalf of Nineteen Applicants, p. 70.

11 *That presumed good faith was promptly breached*
Luard, *History of the United Nations*, 1: 74–78.

CHAPTER 2

13 *the text of which is appended*
McCarran Hearings, Appendix D.2.

13 *It was the particular concern*
McCarran Hearings, pp. 336–37, 412, 416–22.

14 *I had been nothing less*
Trygve Lie, *In the Cause of Peace* (New York: Macmillan, 1954), p. 17.

14 *Under a "cover plan"*
McCarran Hearings, pp. 55, 353, 419; Lie, *In the Cause of Peace*, p. 389.

15 *In the same vein*
McCarran Hearings, pp. 373, 417.

15 *Hickerson had been*
McCarran Hearings, p. 372; obituary, New York *Times*, Jan. 20, 1989.

15 *at least forty*
New York *Times*, Nov. 13, 1952; Jan. 4, 1953. U.N. document A/2364, Jan. 30, 1953, Annex II; Judgements of the United Nations Administrative Tribunal, nos. 1–70, 1950–57 (U.N. document AT/D/EC/1–70), p. 220. Mc-Carran Hearings, pp. 355, 385.

16 *Colleagues and staff representatives*
U.N. document SCC/111, Mar. 19, 1951; *Daily Compass*, Feb. 15, 1951; New York *Post*, Feb. 16, 1951; New York *Herald Tribune*, Feb. 16, 23, 1951; New York *Times*, Feb. 16, 17, 1951.

16 *compensation from the Administrative Tribunal*
Judgements of the United Nations Administrative Tribunal, nos. 1–70, 1950–57 (U.N. document AT/DEC/1–70).

16 *referral of the matter*
Thomas M. Franck, *Nation Against Nation* (New York: Oxford University Press, 1985), pp. 99–100; New York *Times*, June 11, 1954. General Assembly resolution 785 (VIII), Dec. 9, 1953.

16 *being made public*
U.S. News & World Report, Oct. 16, 1953. See also ibid., Dec. 5, 1952.

16 *upheld the ruling*
Advisory Opinion of the International Court of Justice, July 13, 1954; *I.C.J. Reports*, 1954, pp. 47–63; U.N. document SCC/181, July 19, 1954; New York *Times*, July 14, 1954. See also Brian Urquhart, *Hammarskjold* (New York: Knopf, 1972), pp. 68–70.

17 *the administration's stated claim*
Judgements of the United Nations Administrative Tribunal, nos. 1–70, 1950–57 (U.N. document AT/DEC/1–70), p. 48.

17 *Boudin said in 1989*
Statement prepared by the late Leonard B. Boudin and provided to author for this account.

CHAPTER 3

19 *may be estimated*
Author's assessment, based on inquiries and published accounts.

19 *an "efficiency survey"*
U.N. document A/2364, Jan. 30, 1953, Annex II; U.N. Note to Correspondents no. 464, June 6, 1952, p. 10-z; U.N. document SCC/152, Dec. 1, 1952.

19 *a panel of three jurists*
U.N. press release ORG/231, Nov. 29, 1952; Brief on Behalf of Nineteen Applicants, pp. 123–47.

20 *Lie was in fact obliged*
Lie, *In the Cause of Peace*, p. 406.

20 *Three days later*
New York *Times*, Nov. 14, 1952; U.N. press release SG/268, Nov. 13, 1952; Lie, *In the Cause of Peace*, p. 399.

20 *Ralph Bunche, then*
New York *Times*, Nov. 14, 1952.

20 *In later years*
Bunche's view related to author by the colleague to whom it was conveyed.

20 *Shaken by Feller's death*
New York *Times*, Nov. 19, 21, 1952.

20 *Less than a month earlier*
McCarran Hearings, p. 126; meeting of Oct. 15, 1952.

21 *In 1987, in his book*
Julian Behrstock, *The Eighth Case: Troubled Times at the United Nations* (Lanham, Md.: University Press of America, 1987), pp. 31–32.

21 *In a letter regarding Feller's death*
Letter from Professor Telford Taylor, New York *Times*, Nov. 16, 1952.

21 *Hugh Keenleyside*
McCarran Hearings, pp. 17, 18, 20; meeting of Oct. 13, 1952. Also, recollection of author. See Hugh L. Keenleyside, *Memoirs* (Toronto: McClelland, Stewart, 1982), Vol. II, pp. 368–72.

22 *In Europe, however, prominent newspapers*
Brief on Behalf of Nineteen Applicants, pp. 287–300.

22 *certain British and Canadian officials*
Event related to author by one of the participants.

22 *Since, in 1945, Eden himself*
Robert Rhodes James, *Anthony Eden* (London: Weidenfeld & Nicolson, 1986), p. 312.

22 *Discussing, in his memoirs*
Anthony Eden, *The Memoirs of Anthony Eden: Full Circle* (Boston: Houghton Mifflin, 1960), pp. 23–26.

22 *Writing in* Le Monde
Maurice Duverger, "Etats-Unis et Nations unies," *Le Monde*, Nov. 22, 1952.

23 *In his autobiography*
Brian Urquhart, *A Life in Peace and War* (New York: Harper & Row, 1987), p. 122.

23 *overwhelmingly confirms that*
Brief on Behalf of Nineteen Applicants, p. 84.

24 *"the atmosphere of Greek tragedy"*
Lie, *In the Cause of Peace*, p. 398.

24 *a prominent American appellant*
Judgements of the United Nations Administrative Tribunal, nos. 1–70, 1950–57: Judgement no. 31, pp. 135–43.

25 *Dag Hammarskjöld would concede*
Dag Hammarskjöld, Servant of Peace: A Selection of His Speeches and Statements, ed. Wilder Foote (New York: Harper & Row, 1963), p. 300.

25 *In 1989, he related*
Statement prepared by Jack Sargent Harris and provided to author for this account.

26 *recounted by James Barros*
James Barros, *Trygve Lie and the Cold War* (De Kalb: Northern Illinois University Press, 1989), pp. 321–42.

26 *In the new year of 1953*
Lie, *In the Cause of Peace*, pp. 402–3.

27 *the fourth Secretary-General*
U.N. document SCB/470, Nov. 21, 1978.

27 *"You try to get as many posts"*
New York *Times*, Feb. 19, 1985.

28 *large subsidies from their respective governments*
U.N. staff publication entitled *U.N. Report*, October 1988, pp. 4–5; Statement on Supplementary Payments made to the International Civil Service Commission on Behalf of the Coordinating Committee for Independent [U.N.] Staff Unions and Associations, New York, Aug. 24, 1989; New York *Times*, Feb. 19, 1985, p. 2.

28 *"This book is my religion"*
New York *Times*, Sept. 8, 1982.

28 *The provision, inaugurated*
Lie, *In the Cause of Peace*, pp. 402–13; New York *Times*,

Jan. 10, 11, 27, 1953, and Feb. 5, 1953; Urquhart, *Hammarskjold*, pp. 62–63.

28 *some procedural modification*
Franck, *Nation Against Nation*, p. 102.

28 *challenge to its legality*
United States District Court of Massachusetts: *Ozonoff* v. *Berzak*. Civil action no. 71-1046-MC. Plaintiff's Memorandum of Law in Opposition to Motion to Dismiss; Leonard B. Boudin, June 13, 1974.

28 *the clearance was ruled unconstitutional*
United States Court of Appeals for the First Circuit, no. 85-1850. *David Ozonoff, Plaintiff, Appellee,* v. *William P. Berzak, Et Al., Defendants, Appellants.* Appeal from the United States District Court for the District of Massachusetts (Hon. John J. McNaught, U.S. District Judge), Judgment *Affirmed,* Sept. 21, 1984.

28 *An appeal of the court's ruling*
In the United States Court of Appeals for the First Circuit, no. 83-1850, *Ozonoff* v. *Berzak*, Brief for Appellants, January 30, 1984; and no. 85-1850, Brief for Appellee, Mar. 14, 1984.

28 *a subsequent legal challenge*
United States District Court for the Eastern District of Pennsylvania, *William H. Hinton* v. *Donald J. Devine, Et Al.,* Apr. 8, 1986. The Court ordered, inter alia, that: Executive Order 10422, as amended, is declared to be unconstitutional. Civil action no. 84-1130, Apr. 8, 1986.

29 *a branch office*
Lie, *In the Cause of Peace*, pp. 402–3; U.N. document SCC/154, Feb. 16, 1953; Urquhart, *Hammarskjold*, pp. 63–64.

29 *as Hammarskjöld confirmed*
U.N. document SCC/172, Jan. 20, 1954; Conor Cruise

O'Brien, *Writers and Politics* (New York: Vintage, 1967), pp. 210–11; Urquhart, *Hammarskjold*, pp. 63–64.

29 *of a junior employee*
Judgements of the United Nations Administrative Tribunal, nos. 1–70, 1950–57, pp. 192–99; New York *Times,* Sept. 2, 1953; New York *Herald Tribune,* Sept. 2, 1953.

29 *"On what might be called"*
O'Brien, *Writers and Politics,* p. 211.

29 *evidently incomprehensible*
Behrstock, *Eighth Case,* p. 31.

30 *As the chairman of the Foreign Relations Committee*
J. William Fulbright, "In Thrall to Fear," *The New Yorker,* Jan. 8, 1972, p. 60.

30 *Senator Daniel Patrick Moynihan*
New York *Times Book Review,* Feb. 17, 1985, p. 24.

30 *"It is not a United Nations"*
Alexander Solzhenitsyn, *One Word of Truth: The Nobel Speech* (London: Bodley Head, 1972), p. 21.

31 *An official proclamation*
Report on Standards of Conduct in the International Civil Service, 1954. U.N. document COORD/Civil Service/5; see also Urquhart, *Hammarskjold,* p. 69.

32 *Speaking, in 1936*
Winston S. Churchill, *The Second World War,* vol. 1, *The Gathering Storm* (Boston: Houghton Mifflin, 1948), p. 209.

32 *what Dag Hammarskjöld called*
Dag Hammarskjöld, *Servant of Peace,* p. 51.

33 *These revised rules also stated*
Staff Regulations of the United Nations: currently, U.N. document ST/SGB/Staff Regulations/rev. 14, art. 9, reg. 9.1(c).

34 *In refusing to appeal*
New York *Times*, Apr. 3, 1975.

34 *On the same theme*
International Herald Tribune, Apr. 8, 1975.

35 *In 1935, the League of Nations High Commissioner*
Letter of resignation of James G. McDonald, High Commissioner for Refugees (Jewish and Other) Coming from Germany, Dec. 27, 1935: League of Nations document C.13.M.12.1936.XII, annex.

36 *an unidentified U.N. official*
New York *Times*, Apr. 1, 1975.

CHAPTER 4

37 *Byron Price stated*
Administrative circular, Oct. 2, 1950; Brief on Behalf of Nineteen Applicants, p. 223.

38 *he declared*
U.N. document SCC/152, Dec. 1, 1952, p. 7; Brief on Behalf of Nineteen Applicants, p. 35.

38 *Awarding damages in this case*
Judgements of the United Nations Administrative Tribunal, nos. 1–70, 1950–57, pp. 43–53.

38 *a report on personnel policies*
Report of the Secretary-General on Personnel Policy, U.N. document A/2364, Jan. 30, 1953.

38 *a Soviet representative stated*
Official Records of the United Nations General Assembly, Seventh Session, 418th Plenary Meeting, Mar. 30, 1953, p. 598.

38 *an intervention historic*
Official Records of the United Nations General Assembly, Seventh Session, 418th Plenary Meeting, Mar. 30, 1953, p. 605–8.

40 *the brief, late memoir*
Dag Hammarskjöld, *Castle Hill* (Uppsala: Dag Hammarskjöld Foundation, 1971).

40 *his journal,* Markings
Dag Hammarskjöld, *Markings*, tr. Leif Sjöberg and W. H. Auden, with a foreword by W. H. Auden (New York: Knopf, 1964).

41 *The largest work on Hammarskjöld . . . Urquhart himself explaining*
Urquhart, *Hammarskjold*, Foreword, pp. xi, xii, xiii.

41 *"stupid or malicious people"*
Urquhart, *Hammarskjold*, p. 27.

42 *In his later memoirs*
Brian Urquhart, *A Life in Peace and War* (New York: Harper & Row, 1987), p. 126.

43 *I was one of his under-secretaries*
Duncan Christy, interview with Brian Urquhart, in *M: The Civilized Man*, September, 1986.

43 *placed by the U.N. Charter*
Charter of the United Nations, ch. 15, art. 99.

44 *According to personnel statistics*
U.N. document ACC/1989/PER/R.11, July 20, 1989, pp. 15, 16.

45 *Hammarskjöld sought and largely obtained*
U.N. documents A/2533, Nov. 2, 1953; A/2554, Nov. 12, 1953; A/2731, Sept. 21, 1954. General Assembly resolution 782 (VIII), Dec. 9, 1953. See also Urquhart, *Hammarskjold*, pp. 68–70.

45 *in a searching study*
Claude Julien, "La 'Chasse aux Sorcières' " *Le Monde*, Nov. 19, 20, 1953.

45 *the respected senior French member*
Urquhart, *Hammarskjold*, pp. 77–79.

47 *as a matter of urgency*
Official Records of the United Nations General Assembly,
Seventh Session, 418th Plenary Meeting, Mar. 30, 1953,
p. 608.

47 *he acknowledged, in his eighth year*
Dag Hammarskjöld, Servant of Peace, p. 300.

47 *"between a youngish headmaster"*
Conor Cruise O'Brien, *To Katanga and Back: A U.N.*
Case History (New York: Simon & Schuster, 1962), p. 51.

47 *the analogy of a school*
New York *Times,* Aug. 9, 1988.

48 *a long personal letter of dismissal*
U.N. press release SG/700, July 3, 1958. See also Hazzard, *Defeat of an Ideal,* pp. 184–89, 275–77.

48 *a disciplinary body*
U.N. Note to Correspondents no. 1840, July 9, 1958. See
also Urquhart, *Hammarskjold,* pp. 244–48.

49 *an admiring article*
Madeleine G. Kalb, "The U.N.'s Embattled Peacekeeper," New York *Times Magazine,* Dec. 19, 1982,
pp. 42ff.

CHAPTER 5

50 *The exhortation*
Report of the Headquarters Commission to the Second Part
of the First Session of the General Assenbly of the United
Nations, October, 1946, U.N. document A/69, p. 27.

50 *a picture by Courbet*
Gerstle Mack, *Gustave Courbet* (New York: Knopf, 1951):
plate no. 41, pp. 176–77; Jack Lindsay, *Gustave Courbet:*
His Life and Art (London: Jupiter Books, 1973),
pp. 181–82.

51 *the Preparatory Commission*
U.N. document PC/20, ch. 8, sec. 2, par. 67.

51 *individual ex-gratia payments*
"Move to Oust Briton," *Observer*, Dec. 23, 1984, p. 1;
"S-G Won't Let Urquhart Fully Retire from the U.N.,"
Diplomatic World Bulletin, Jan. 14, 1985, p. 1.

51 *and in the field*
See Graham Hancock, *Lords of Poverty* (New York: Atlantic Monthly Press, 1989).

52 *An analogy—frequently drawn*
Executive Budget of the City of New York for the Fiscal Year 1990.

52 *an exposition by Ronald Kessler*
Washington *Post*, June 17, 18, 19, 1979; New York *Times*, June 20, 1979; U.N. press release, note no. 4160, June 21, 1979.

53 *Following the* Post's *study*
U.S. News & World Report, Sept. 17, 1979, p. 63.

53 *The official total*
U.N. document ACC/1989/PER/R.11, July 20, 1989, pp. 8, 10.

54 *The transfer to United Nations custody*
New York *Times*, July 15, 25, 30, 1972.

54 *Shortly after his election*
See Urquhart, *Hammarskjold*, p. 55, and relevant notes.

54 *the comment of Cato the Censor*
Cicero, *De Divinatione*, II, xxiv.

55 *In 1977, a detailed study*
U.S. Senate, Committee on Government Operations: U.S. Participation in International Organizations (Abraham

Ribicoff, Chairman), document no. 95-50, February, 1977 (stock no. 052-071-00525-1).

Chapter 6

56 *Jakobson himself commented*
Flora Lewis, in New York *Times*, Apr. 24, 1986.

56 *Among prominent commentators*
Joseph Kraft, "A New Man at the U.N.," Boston *Globe*, Dec. 27, 1971.

57 *Announcing Waldheim's election*
New York *Times*, Dec. 22, 1971.

58 *a subsequent article*
"Week in Review," New York *Times*, Dec. 26, 1971.

60 *Questioned on the theme*
New York *Times*, Apr. 25, 1986.

60 *In his book*
Robert E. Herzstein, *Waldheim: The Missing Years* (New York: Arbor House/William Morrow, 1988), p. 257.

60 *the Austrian authorities also requested*
Kurt Waldheim's Wartime Years: A Documentation (Vienna: Carl Gerold's Sohn, 1987), p. 11.

61 *Gruber has related*
Kurt Waldheim's Wartime Years, pp. 131–32; New York *Times*, Apr. 25, 26, 1986.

61 *In his book* Waldheim and Austria
Richard Bassett, *Waldheim and Austria* (New York: Viking Penguin, 1989), p. 68.

61 *Fritz Molden, who had been*
Herzstein, *Waldheim: The Missing Years*, pp. 167–72.

62 *Karl Gruber has said*
New York *Times*, Apr. 25, 26, 1986.

62 *Waldheim accounted for his enrollment*
Herzstein, *Waldheim: The Missing Years*, p. 175.

63 *the older Waldheim . . . Waldheim's repeated assertion*
Kurt Waldheim, *In the Eye of the Storm: A Memoir* (Bethesda, Md.: Adler & Adler, 1986), pp. 16–17; Herzstein, *Waldheim: The Missing Years*, p. 55; Washington *Post*, Jan. 18, 1980; Jane Rosen, "Man in the Middle," New York *Times Magazine*, Sept. 13, 1981; New York *Times*, Dec. 22, 1971; Hillel Seidman, *United Nations: Perfidy and Perversion* (New York: M. P. Press, 1982), pp. 54–56.

63 *in the early nineteen-fifties*
Herzstein, *Waldheim: The Missing Years*, p. 259.

63 *In August, 1988*
New York *Times*, Aug. 19, 1988.

63 *In November, 1989*
Washington *Post*, Nov. 30, 1989; New York *Times*, Nov. 30, 1989.

63 *Herzstein's comment*
Herzstein, *Waldheim: The Missing Years*, p. 222.

64 *archives on war criminals . . . in American archives*
Michael Palumbo, *The Waldheim Files* (London: Faber & Faber, 1988); New York *Times*, Apr. 12, 25, 26, and May 15, 1986; Herzstein, *Waldheim: The Missing Years*, ch. 16.

64 *assertions would be made*
New York *Times*, June 4, 5, 6, 7, 1986; *Times* (London), May 25, 1988; Herzstein, *Waldheim: The Missing Years*, pp. 227–31.

64 *George Bush*
New York *Times*, Dec. 22, 1971.

65 *The new Secretary-General*
Editorial, *Times* (London), Dec. 23, 1971.

66 *On the last day*
New York *Times,* Dec. 31, 1971.

67 *From 1967 on . . . voiced support for the criticisms*
See Hazzard, *Defeat of an Ideal,* pp. 92–93, 265; *Guardian,* Nov. 7, 1967; *Bulletin of the Atomic Scientists,* February, 1971, p. 43.

67 *In 1969*
A Study of the Capacity of the United Nations Development System, vols. 1 and 2 combined, U.N. document DP/5 (Geneva, 1969).

68 *"some prehistoric monster"*
Study of the Capacity of the United Nations Development System, p. iii.

68 *and a lengthy article*
Hugh L. Keenleyside, "What's Wrong at the United Nations," *Saturday Review,* June 19, 1971, pp. 11–13, 29–30.

68 *a report on personnel problems*
Personnel Questions: Report of the Joint Inspection Unit on Personnel Problems in the United Nations, U.N. document A/8454 (Parts I and II), Oct. 5, 1971; hereinafter cited as JIU.

69 *a claim that the organization's usefulness*
See Hazzard, *Defeat of an Ideal,* ch. 6.

CHAPTER 7

73 *surprised his sponsors*
See *The Memoirs of Lord Gladwyn* (London: Weidenfeld & Nicolson, 1972), p. 257; Brian Urquhart, "International Peace and Security," *Foreign Affairs,* Fall, 1981, p. 1–2.

73 *he informed the world*
Cited in Washington *Post,* Jan. 18, 1980. See Anthony

Astrachan, "Waldheim: Learning the Uses of Limited Power," *Saturday Review/World,* Mar. 23, 1974, pp. 12–13.

74 *the representative of France*
Official Records of the United Nations General Assembly, Seventh Session, 418th Plenary Meeting, Mar. 30, 1953, p. 608. See also Urquhart, *Hammarskjold,* p. 81: view of Thanassis Agnides, Chairman, U.N. Advisory Committee on Administrative and Budgetary Questions.

74 *a study highly critical*
Seymour Maxwell Finger and John Mugno, *The Politics of Staffing the United Nations Secretariat* (New York: Ralph Bunche Institute on the United Nations of the City University of New York, 1974); New York *Times,* Jan. 11, 1975; New York *Post,* Jan. 10, 1975.

74 *Although the Secretary-General*
Finger and Mugno, *Politics of Staffing the United Nations Secretariat,* p. 22.

74 *a "restructuring" . . . as "historic"*
A New United Nations Structure for Global Economic Cooperation, U.N. document E/AC.62/9, May 28, 1975; New York *Times,* May 21, 1975.

75 *in Gibbon's words*
Edward Gibbon, *The History of the Decline and Fall of the Roman Empire,* ch. 37.

76 *In 1971, the Joint Inspection Unit*
JIU, pp. 51–53.

CHAPTER 8

78 *Waldheim called on*
Waldheim, *In the Eye of the Storm,* pp. 41–42; New York *Times,* Dec. 20, 1972.

78 *the New York* Times *reported*
New York *Times*, Dec. 10, 1985.

78 *In 1973*
New York *Times*, Sept. 11, 1973. See also New York *Times*, Nov. 10, 1977.

78 *Waldheim's own attitude*
New York *Times*, Dec. 20, 1972.

78 *cited the proposal*
Editorial, "Back to the Stone Age," New York *Times*, Dec. 20, 1972.

79 *Urquhart criticizes*
Urquhart, *Life in Peace and War*, p. 229.

79 *in a review*
Bernard Nossiter, "Forty Years at the United Nations," Washington *Post Book World*, Sept. 27, 1987.

79 *Commenting in 1981*
Brian Urquhart, "International Peace and Security," *Foreign Affairs*, Fall, 1981, p. 14.

80 *U Thant, in an opening address*
U.N. document A/CONF.32/41: *Final Act of the International Conference on Human Rights, Teheran, Apr. 22 to May 13, 1968*; Annex II, *Addresses delivered at the opening of the Conference*, p. 34.

80 *acknowledged, in January, 1980*
ABC News, "Issues and Answers" (Barbara Walters), Jan. 6, 1980.

80 *he had asserted*
Introduction to the Report of the Secretary-General on the Work of the Organization, GAOR(XXVII), supplement no. 1A (A/8701/add.1), August, 1972.

81 *brief and excruciating*
New York *Times*, Mar. 10, 1974.

81 *President Salvador Allende*
New York *Times*, Dec. 5, 1972; editorial, "What Allende
Left Out," New York *Times*, Dec. 9, 1972.

81 *In May, 1979*
Newsweek, May 7, 1979.

81 *in an editorial*
Editorial, *Times* (London), May 18, 1977.

82 *espoused a view*
See Shirley Hazzard, "Where Governments Go to
Church," *New Republic*, Mar. 1, 1975, p. 13. Document
cited in author's possession.

82 *was publicly deplored*
Letter from John P. Humphrey, New York *Times*, Mar. 20,
1977.

82 *Speaking, in 1957*
Martin Gilbert, *Winston S. Churchill: Never Despair
(1945–1965)* (Boston: Houghton Mifflin, 1988), p. 1249.

82 *Brian Urquhart, who*
"On Slamming the U.N." (transcript of television program
"World Chronicle"), *United Nations Secretariat News*,
Mar. 31, 1982.

82 *praised the organization*
Interview with Brian Urquhart in *M: The Civilized Man*,
September, 1986, pp. 156–60.

83 *van Boven's statement*
New York *Times*, Feb. 11, 1982.

84 Times *of London observed*
Editorial, *Times* (London), Jan. 30, 1989. See also "Week
in Review," New York *Times*, Dec. 8, 1985.

84 *"when the vote was announced"*
New York *Times*, Mar. 10, 1989.

84 *In August, 1989*
New York *Times*, Aug. 31 and Sept. 1, 1989.

84 *exacerbated a movement*
New York *Times*, Dec. 17, 1989.

85 *was discovered only in 1980*
Report of the Joint Inspection Unit on Evaluation of the
Office of the United Nations Disaster Relief Co-ordinator:
U.N. document A/36/73, Geneva, October, 1980.
　　See also New York *Times*, Nov. 18 and Dec. 9, 1980.
And editorial, New York *Times*, Dec. 21, 1971.

85 *In 1978, in his foreword*
Brian Urquhart, "Foreword," in Thomas W. Oliver, *The
United Nations in Bangladesh* (Princeton: Princeton Uni-
versity Press, 1978), pp. vii–viii.

86 *a confidential report by Toni Hagen*
Toni Hagen, *Report on U.N. Relief Operations, Bangladesh* (December, 1971–June, 1972), Parts 1 and 2, U.N.
document GE-72-8880.

86 *Thomas Oliver, who describes Hagen*
Oliver, *United Nations in Bangladesh*, pp. 100, 101, 121,
128, 193.

88 *a leading United Nations representative in Cyprus*
New York *Times*, Sept. 16, 1979; *International Herald
Tribune*, Oct. 27–28, 1979.

88 *Ten years later, in 1989*
New York *Times*, Oct. 5, 1989; *International Herald
Tribune*, Oct. 26, 1989.

CHAPTER 9

89 *his appeal for protection*
New York *Times*, July 25, 1972.

89 *Waldheim expressed his gratitude*
New York *Times*, Nov. 22, 1973.

90 *In February of that year*
See account in U.N. press release SG/SM/2033, July 5, 1974.

90 *the United Nations Charter*
Charter of the United Nations, ch. 15, art. 100.

90 *the U.N. Universal Declaration*
Universal Declaration of Human Rights, art. 19.

90 *during a press conference*
See U.N. press release SG/SM/2033, July 5, 1974.

91 *prominently protested*
Shirley Hazzard, "The Guest Word," New York *Times Book Review*, Aug. 25, 1974. See also "Letters," New York *Times Book Review*, Sept. 22 and Oct. 6, 1974, and *Times* (London), July 2, 1974. In addition, correspondence concerning this episode in author's possession.

91 *as Foreign Minister*
Herzstein, *Waldheim: The Missing Years*, p. 222.

91 *so much as an appeal*
New York *Times*, Apr. 3, 1975; *International Herald Tribune*, Apr. 8, 1975.

91 *his notable condemnation*
Inter alia, Rosen, "Man in the Middle."

91 *apparent endorsement*
New York *Times*, July 24, 1979. See also New York *Times*, Mar. 5, 1979, and Apr. 25, 1981.

92 *between Egypt and Israel*
New York *Times*, Feb. 3, 1978. See also New York *Times*, Jan. 12, 1978, and Dec. 22, 1980.

92 *in its first reference*
New York *Times*, June 9, 1986.

92 *Joseph Kraft's 1971 observation*
Kraft, "A New Man at the U.N."

93 *United Nations peace medal*
Times (London), Sept. 13, 1977.

93 *his favors were evenly distributed*
New York *Times*, June 15, 1986.

94 *his disparagement*
International Herald Tribune, Apr. 8, 1975.

94 *the Western press*
New York *Times*, June 7, 1986. See also Washington *Post*,
Oct. 30, 1986; New York *Times*, Oct. 31, 1986.

94 *Waldheim's Balkan history*
New York *Times*, June 15, 1986.

94 *words of George Eliot*
George Eliot, *Felix Holt, the Radical*, ch. 29.

CHAPTER 10

95 *"In terms of usefulness"*
Rosen, "Man in the Middle."

96 *given currency by Bismarck*
Otto von Bismarck, speech to the Reichstag on the eastern
crisis, Feb. 19, 1878. See A. J. P. Taylor, *Bismarck: The
Man and the Statesman* (New York: Vintage, 1955),
p. 170.

96 *"a great fashion for slamming"*
"On Slamming the U.N."

97 *In an interview*
Kalb, "U.N.'s Embattled Peacekeeper."

97 *tenets for peacekeeping*
Editorial, New York *Times*, Jan. 28, 1986.

97 *"All I have is moral power"*
Times (London), July 9, 1977.

98 *in his respective prefaces*
Brian Urquhart, "Preface," in Kurt Waldheim, *The Challenge of Peace* (London: Weidenfeld & Nicolson, 1980), pp. vii, viii, ix; Brian Urquhart, "Foreword" in Kurt Waldheim, *Building the Future Order* (New York: Free Press, 1980), pp. xi, xii, xiii.

98 *the Washington* Post *reported*
Myra MacPherson, "Waldheim, the U.N.'s Silent Peacekeeper," Washington *Post*, Jan. 18, 1980.

98 *"Waffle, but Still Worthwhile"*
Times (London), Oct. 6, 1984.

98 *"When Nothing Is Better than Nothing"*
Times (London), Oct. 23, 1985. See also *New Republic*, Nov. 4, 1985.

99 *A later article by O'Brien*
Conor Cruise O'Brien, "At the Shrine of Honourable Failure," *Times Literary Supplement*, Nov. 6–12, 1987.

101 *And, in February, 1982*
New York *Times*, Feb. 10, 1982.

CHAPTER 11

102 *an extensive appreciation*
Times Literary Supplement, Jan. 17, 1986. See also Conor Cruise O'Brien, *Passion and Cunning* (New York: Simon & Schuster, 1988), p. 7.

104 *Hammarskjöld had addressed himself*
Dag Hammarskjöld, *Servant of Peace*, p. 149.

105 *Brian Urquhart had decried*
Rosen, "Man in the Middle."

CHAPTER 12

107 *a United States representative*
United States Mission to the United Nations, press release
USUN-112(76), Oct. 11, 1976: *Statement by Mrs. Ersa H.
Poston, U.S. Representative in Committee 5, on the Compo-
sition of the Secretariat.* See also New York *Times,* Oct. 12,
13, 1976.

107 *greeted the event warmly*
New York *Times,* Dec. 8, 1976.

108 *The documented account*
Records of the United Nations Staff Union, 1976–1981,
with particular reference to document series SCB. See also
U.N. document A/C.5/33/CRP.7, Dec. 7, 1978: *Person-
nel Questions (Statement by the Chairman of the Staff
Committee to the Members of the Fifth Committee of the
General Assembly);* and document SCB/478, Jan. 3, 1979.

109 *in his book*
Theodor Meron, *The United Nations Secretariat: The Rules
and the Practice* (Lexington, Mass.: Lexington Books,
1977). See also Theodor Meron, "Waldheim, His Office,
and Its Future," New York *Times,* Oct. 26, 1981.

109 *which he likened . . . "he honors it"*
Washington *Post,* Feb. 18, 1979. See also New York
Times, Feb. 5, 1979.

109 *"The thing that utterly amazed me"*
Conversation with author.

110 *"Waldheim would be"*
Conversation with author. See Shirley Hazzard, "The
League of Frightened Men," *New Republic,* Jan. 19, 1980.

110 *The correspondence between*
Records of Battle, Fowler, Jaffin, Pierce, and Kheel, New
York City.

110 *Kheel has observed*
Conversation with author.

111 *human rights in Poland*
See Franck, *Nation Against Nation*, pp. 235–36, 238, 241–42. See also New York *Times*, Dec. 15, 1981, and Jan. 10, 1982.

111 *a crowded rally*
U.N. Staff Union document SCB/531, Jan. 23, 1980. See also SCB/470, Nov. 21, 1978; SCB/517, Nov. 2, 1979; SCB/659, Nov. 3, 1982.

111 *two months later*
New York *Times*, Feb. 14, 1980. See also New York *Times*, Apr. 10, 1980; *Newsweek*, Mar. 17, 1980; *New Republic*, Sept. 20, 1980.

112 *Following her release*
Account of these events provided to author by Alicja Wesolowska. See also New York *Times*, Mar. 14, 1984.

112 *have apparently tripled*
Information obtained from U.N. staff representatives. See also U.N. staff publication *U.N. Report*, December, 1986, vol. 3, no. 3.

CHAPTER 13

113 *deplored public mention*
Document in author's possession.

114 *an interview in 1975*
Barbara Kerr, "Kurt Waldheim: Mr. U.N. Is Tougher Than Expected," *People*, Feb. 3, 1975.

114 *In his autobiography*
Waldheim, *In the Eye of the Storm*, p. 18.

115 *According to recent research*
Herzstein, *Waldheim: The Missing Years*, pp. 65–66, 229.

116 *makes passing reference*
Waldheim, *In the Eye of the Storm*, p. 15.

116 *in the "white book"*
Kurt Waldheim's Wartime Years, p. 12.

116 *"harassed continuously"*
Washington *Post*, Jan. 18, 1980.

116 *one of the first*
Seidman, *United Nations: Perfidy and Perversion*, pp. 55–56.

117 *Waldheim met his future wife*
Waldheim, *Challenge of Peace*, p. 25.

117 *Waldheim was apparently*
Herzstein, *Waldheim: The Missing Years*, pp. 98–99, 236, 252. See also the New York *Times*, Mar. 6, 1986; and *Times Literary Supplement*, Mar. 4–10, 1988.

117 *as she acknowledged*
New York *Times*, June 12, 1986. See also Herzstein, *Waldheim: The Missing Years*, pp. 81, 113.

117 *In April, 1943*
Herzstein, *Waldheim: The Missing Years*, p. 83.

118 *"a man who once said"*
Washington *Post*, Jan. 18, 1980: statement by Waldheim appears in Waldheim, *Challenge of Peace*, p. 8.

118 Our Mutual Friend
Charles Dickens, *Our Mutual Friend*, bk. 2, ch. 4.

CHAPTER 14

119 *On November 26, 1980*
Letter from Stephen J. Solarz to Kurt Waldheim, Nov. 26, 1980: records of Congressman Solarz, no. 43777, document no. 15594, category code 1615, 32110. Correspondence reproduced in Seidman, *United Nations: Perfidy and Perversion*, pp. 145–50.

119 *in* The New Republic
Hazzard, "League of Frightened Men."

119 *a further assertion*
M.P., "Cambridge Diarist," *New Republic*, Sept. 27, 1980, p. 43.

119 *On December 19th*
Letter from Kurt Waldheim to Stephen J. Solarz, Dec. 19, 1980. Records of Congressman Solarz, as above.

119 *had characterized*
See letter from Robert Ratner, President of the United Nations Association of the United States of America, *New Republic*, Feb. 16, 1980, p. 4.

120 *In March, 1986*
International Herald Tribune, Mar. 10, 1986. See also New York *Times*, Mar. 6 and Apr. 26, 1986.

121 *an uncompromising article*
M.P., "Washington Diarist," *New Republic*, Mar. 7, 1981, p. 42.

121 *Peretz has recounted*
M.P., "Washington Diarist," *New Republic*, June 23, 1986, p. 43. See also *New Republic*, Apr. 28, 1986.

121 *In his memoirs*
Waldheim, *In the Eye of the Storm*, p. 40.

121 *Solarz would again write*
Letter from Stephen J. Solarz to Kurt Waldheim, Apr. 1, 1986: records of Congressman Solarz, as above.

121 *would receive a reply*
Letter from Kurt Waldheim to Stephen J. Solarz, Apr. 21, 1986: records of Congressman Solarz, as above.

121 *On December 31, 1980*
Letter from Frederick P. Hitz to Stephen J. Solarz, Dec. 31, 1980: records of Congressman Solarz, as above.

Reproduced in Seidman, *United Nations: Perfidy and Perversion*, p. 149.

122 *Graham Greene*
Letter from Graham Greene to Shirley Hazzard, Jan. 17, 1981, in author's possession.

122 *In October, 1979*
Guardian editorial reproduced in *International Herald Tribune*, Oct. 20–21, 1979.

CHAPTER 15

123 *In the summer*
New York *Times*, July 14, 1981.

123 Pravda *coupled his name*
New York *Times*, July 14, 1981. See also James Reston, "The Ideal Diplomat," New York *Times*, Sept. 23, 1981.

123 *had reported concern*
New York *Times*, Nov. 19, 1981.

124 *"no personal prejudice"*
New York *Times*, Dec. 4, 1981. See also New York *Times*, Nov. 28, 1981.

124 *Conor Cruise O'Brien*
Times Literary Supplement, Jan. 17, 1986.

124 *"His favorite word"*
New York *Times*, Dec. 12, 1981.

124 *In 1983, Waldheim helped*
New York *Times*, Apr. 28, 1985.

125 *the Austrian magazine* Profil . . . *The following day*
Profil, Mar. 3, 1986. See also *Profil*, Aug. 24, 1987. New York *Times*, Mar. 4, 1986. *Times* (London), Mar. 5, 1986.

125 *Of these disclosures*
New York *Times*, Mar. 4, 1986. See also New York *Times*,
Mar. 6, 1986.

125 *now responded*
New York *Times*, Mar. 4, 1986.

125 *"too boring"*
Times (London), Mar. 31, 1986.

126 *he later observed*
New York *Times*, Apr. 17, 1986.

126 *Anthony Trollope observed*
Anthony Trollope, *Mr. Scarborough's Family*, ch. 5.

CHAPTER 16

127 *"insatiable ambition"* . . . *"monstrous ego"* . . . *"hide of a
rhinoceros"*
Newsweek, June 9, 1986.

127 *"fantasies"*
Urquhart, *Life in Peace and War*, p. 228.

127 *has related elsewhere*
"Letters," New York *Times Book Review*, May 1, 1988.

128 *two notable condemnations*
"Letters," *Independent*, Mar. 24 and 25, 1988. See also
Independent, Mar. 21; *Times* (London), Aug. 10, 1988;
and *Times Literary Supplement*, Mar. 4–10, 1988.

131 *discuss with some detachment*
O'Brien, *To Katanga and Back*, p. 50.

131 *O'Brien then candidly recounted*
O'Brien, *To Katanga and Back*, p. 299.

CHAPTER 17

133 *In* The Quality of Mercy
William Shawcross, *The Quality of Mercy* (New York: Simon & Schuster, 1984), p. 428.

134 *greeted as "success"*
New York *Times*, Aug. 14, 1988.

134 *in James Merrill's words*
James Merrill, "Bronze," in *Late Settings* (New York: Atheneum, 1985), p. 55.

134 *embraced by Dag Hammarskjöld*
Dag Hammarskjöld, Servant of Peace, p. 149.

135 *in a document entitled*
Joint Inspection Unit, *Some Reflections on Reform of the United Nations*. Prepared by Maurice Bertrand. JIU/REP/ 85/9, Geneva 1985. (Covering document: A/40/988, Dec. 6, 1985.) See also *Times* (London), Oct. 1, 1985.

136 *the words are Milton's*
John Milton, "Of Reformation touching Church-Discipline in England," in *John Milton: Selected Prose*, p. 89.

136 *Conor Cruise O'Brien reports*
Times Literary Supplement, Jan. 17, 1986.

INDEX

167

McCarthyism and, 17, 20, 23–
24, 26, 31–32, 73–74
major states' perception of, 5
national candidates in, 27
Nazism and, 6
New York *Times* on, 66, 78,
101
O'Brien on, 99, 131
operating costs of, 52
origins of, 3–5
Parsons on, 99
passivity of, 122
peacekeeping and, 68–69
postwar era and, 100
press and, 67
Price's influence of, 13, 16, 33
public funds wasted by, 54–55
public perception of, 77–78,
85, 86–87, 88, 95, 96–97,
128, 132, 134
reform attempted at, 107–8
reforms urged for, 68, 134–36
restructuring in, 74–75
salaries in, 50, 51, 53, 55
schism in, 24, 31
secret dossiers in, 75
Solzhenitsyn censored by, 90–
91
Solzhenitsyn on, 30
Soviet dissidents and, 81
Soviet Union and, 10–11, 110
staff of, 53
staff rally in, 111
terrorism and, 78
Urquhart on, 96
U.S. and, 6–9, 12, 14–18,
23–24, 27, 32–33, 55, 72,
107
U.S. State Department and, 7,
8, 14–15

utility of, 100–1
Vietnam refugees and, 34, 35–
36
Vietnam War and, 69–70, 78
Waldheim and, 6, 107, 130–32
War Crimes archive of, 59
Wesolowska episode and,
110–12
women's rights and, 44
*United Nations: Perfidy and
Perversion* (Seidman),
116–17
United Nations Administrative
Tribunal, 6
compensation awarded by, 16–
18, 24, 38
Hammarskjöld and, 45
United Nations Advisory Com-
mittee, 130
United Nations Association of the
United States, 119
United Nations Charter, 9, 10–
11, 22, 37, 47, 84, 90
consequences of violating, 26–
28
international civil service and,
45
U.N. Secretariat and, 76
U.S. State Department and,
12, 15
violation of, 7, 11–12, 19, 51,
75
United Nations Commission on
Human Rights, 80–82, 83–
84
London *Times* on, 84
United Nations Development
Programme, 53
United Nations Disaster Relief
Organization (UNDRO), 85